6.99
D0358070
donald MacA
horses,
stones,
Wrecked
cars,
love stories
dog-gone
Books
North Berwick

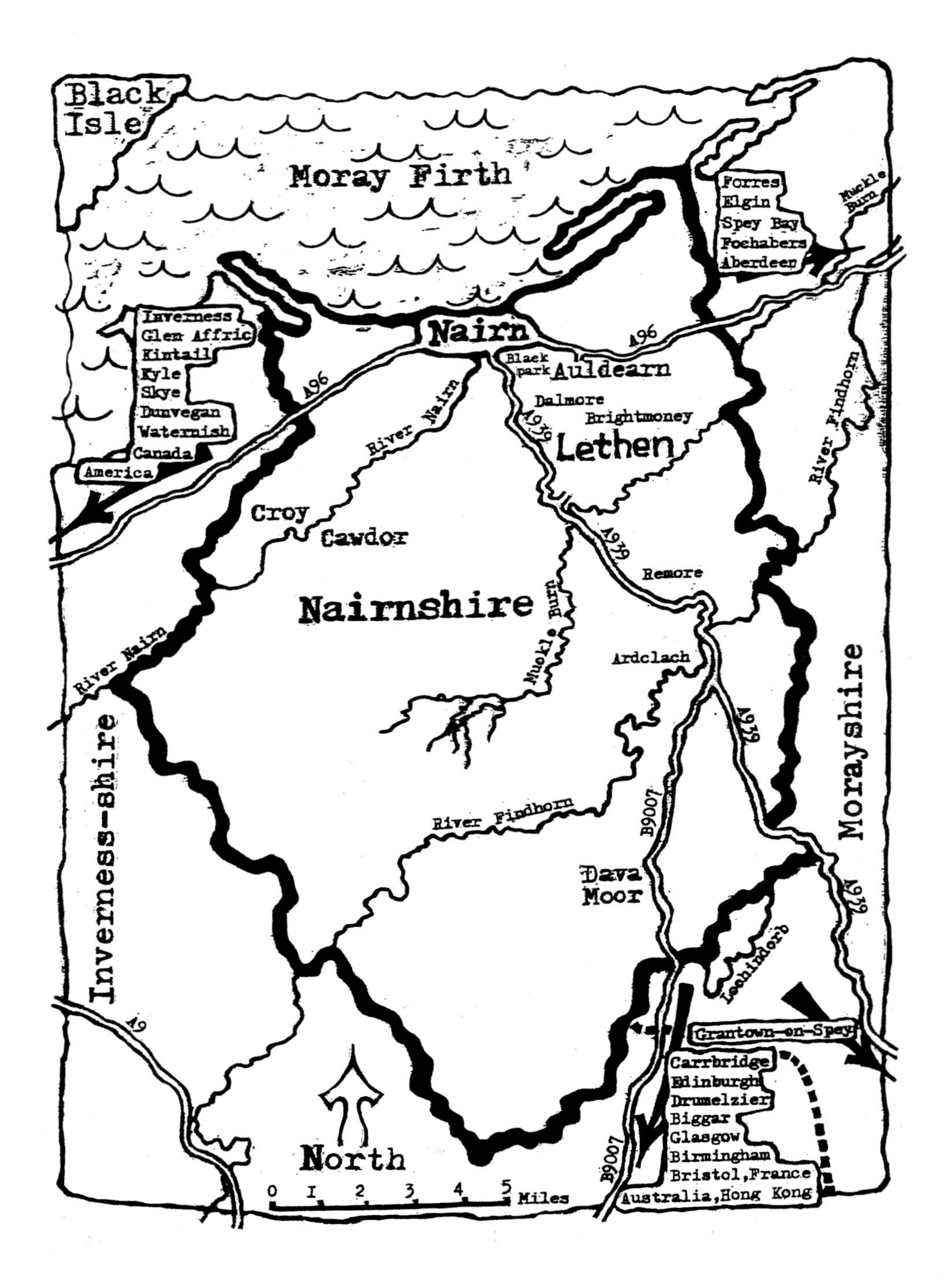

Black Isle
Moray Firth
Forres
Elgin
Spey Bay
Fochabers
Aberdeen
Muckle Burn
Inverness
Glen Affric
Kintail
Kyle
Skye
Dunvegan
Waternish
Canada
America
Nairn
A96
Black park
Auldearn
Dalmore
Brightmoney
A939
Lethen
River Nairn
River Findhorn
Croy
Cawdor
Remore
Nairnshire
Muckle Burn
Ardclach
River Nairn
Inverness-shire
Morayshire
River Findhorn
B9007
Dava Moor
Lochindorb
Grantown-on-Spey
A9
Carrbridge
Edinburgh
Drumelzier
Biggar
Glasgow
Birmingham
Bristol, France
Australia, Hong Kong
North
0 1 2 3 4 5 Miles

To my Mother and Father
Anne (MacArthur) Ker and Jack Ker,
and their friends
Alice (James) Mackintosh and John Mackintosh,
For all the good times,
Talking, laughing and telling stories.

Acknowledgements

To Moira Hewer for vast encouragement, to Marion Smith for making me begin to write, to Rose Little for my first (and only) fan letter. To Commander Lewis-Jones, Fleet Air Arm, for his extraordinary vitality and wisdom. To Mrs Nicol, teacher, Nairn Academy, 1959, for poetry. To Joan Withers, Carole MacIntyre, Ruth Ker, Bebe Ker (wonderful sister), and George Graham (bronze penguin maker supreme) for taking my handwriting into print. To Frances and Dave Cohen and family for feeding me, mind, body, heart and soul since 1968, and to the Mackintosh clan of Blackpark, Nairnshire for sixty years of great acquaintance. To Floss and Alf Dickson, my mother and father-in-law, for Bristol and not divorcing me. To my children, Esther, Daniel and Luke for being (thank God) different from me, and my other wonderful sister Kirsty for her (almost totally) sweet nature. To my Aunts and Uncles from the West, (the Gaelic crowd); Anjey, Lola, Donald, Morag, John, Finlay, Charlie, and from the East, (the Farmers); Annie, Andrew, Astie, Jimmy, and Janet, for all the stories they told, mostly about each other. To Davy and Sheena Reid for dog kennels and caramel wafers, to the Wilkinson family for croquet and inspiration. To Raimond Morganti for friendship and to Anne Morganti for being a Rock and Roll singer. To Maggie Jackson (my beloved sister-in-law, a hippy to the end) for her enthusiasm about absolutely everything. To Jock MacDonald who knew the life story of every blade of grass (and everything else, including me) that grew in Nairnshire, and to Bunty MacDonald, his sister, for the sunny days at Fornighty. To Drew and Trish Fiddes for showing me that a JCB can dance and that football is magic. To Dolores Stewart for her guest appearance, to Jakey Howarth for borrowing his name, and to Lily Bell for being a total treasure. To Meg Sherratt for the story; 'Learning to speak Gaelic', Virginia Medley for 'Drumelzier', Annie Thomas for happiness, sadness and raindrops. To Ramsay Midwood and Randy Weeks for the best live music ever heard in Scotland. To all dogs, especially Lucky, Rusty, Tucker, Malou, One-er, Minnie and Jenna, and to seven cats, Zeus (the puss), Boo, Laya, Moet, Chandon, Hendrix and Tartan. To South Lanarkshire Libraries, Alexander McCall Smith (the judge), Radio 4 and the English Arts Council for their appreciation (and the £300). To all nurses, farmers and workers on the land everywhere always, and to the glorious, amazing, creative, unpredictable, sensational people of Garvald Centre, Edinburgh, who have carried me, dazed and disorientated with the experience, through most of my life.

‘And in my dying hour
When my light begins to fade
Remember that I loved you
Not the promises you made’

'ESTHER'
By RAMSAY MIDWOOD

****

‘Now he fell for a girl who was born misunderstood
In a small car, on the outskirts of town
With a ticket in her window, hair on fire
And the moon was red and thin as a needle
And it fell into the sea, that shimmered, shiny
Like a shark skin suit, whose beauty and splendour
Could never be imagined, even by the most
Industrious of poets’

‘FISHERMAN’S FRIEND’
By RAMSAY MIDWOOD

****

Published by
DOG-GONE BOOKS
Halflinbarns Schoolhouse
Tantallon
North Berwick
EH39 5PW

Although all the places in these stories are real, this is completely a work of fiction
(except for 'Lethen' which might be nearly true)

A CIP catalogue record for this book
is available from the British Library

ISBN – 0-9548994-0-7

Cover and map by Donald MacArthur Ker
Page design by Ruth Ker and George Graham
Gaelic translations by Anjey MacArthur and Rhoda MacLeod
Text in Georgia and Times New Roman

Printed by

MMS Almac Limited
Unit F
Isla Bank Mills
Keith
AB55 5DD

CONTENTS

Learning To Speak Gaelic

Davy thought that maybe Ella had one leg shorter than the other, or it might have been something about her hip, or even some accident or illness she'd had as a child, but whatever it was that made her walk the way she did, the first time he saw her coming along the corridor of the Inverness Midmills College with a group of other students, who tended to stay the same height as they flowed towards him, she bobbed up and down amongst them, rising and falling with each step.

In fact it is likely that Davy would have noticed Ella anyway with her poppy coloured hair, her beads, her emerald and orange clothes, but he remembers it was her locomotion that he first noticed, that first attracted him, the hoppity way she forged along. He was not to discover the exact mechanics of why she walked that way, even after they had been friends for many months. What he did find out, very early in this friendship, was that Ella was very quick to take offence. One night, not long after they had first spoken to each other, they were sitting together after work, drinking, and Davy was thinking how much he liked her nose which was very flat on the bridge, but squarish and uptilted at the end.

He said, "I've broken my nose twice. Have you ever broken yours?"

Because there was a kind of boxer's look to Ella's nose, though beautiful.

And she said, "What's wrong with my nose?"

And he said, "Nothing, nothing, there's nothing wrong with it. It's fine. It's a fine nose. I mean really nice. There's nothing wrong with it. That's not what I meant."

But Ella said, "You've just said it looks like a broken nose. Bloody cheek."

"No, no," said Davy. "I didn't."

"You did," she said. "You implied it. And that's what you meant. Don't lie. God. We're sitting here and I was totally happy and then you have to go and insult me about my nose. Bloody hell. And you are no beauty yourself. Or your nose. But I wouldn't have said it, tried to hurt you like that. Or anything."

"No, no, no. I didn't mean to insult you Ella. I didn't. I would never. I mean it's a beautiful nose. It is. You are. I mean I only said mine was broken, not yours. I'm sorry. I never thought you'd think I was insulting your nose. Definitely not. It's perfect. I've never, and I mean this, seen a more perfect and beautiful nose."

"Ok. Ok then," she said. "I'm not convinced, but alright. I'll try to forget it. But bloody hell."

So Davy had never got round to mentioning her walk. There seemed to be no safe way he could approach the subject.

Davy had come to Inverness from Waternish on the Isle of Skye to do a pre-paramedic, pre-nursing course. Ella was doing the art-portfolio course in the same building. Usually there was no way that Davy would have met Ella. He was shy unless he was so drunk that she would not have wanted to meet him anyway. But that year he got a job three nights a week loading shelves in Safeways. The first night he started he saw that Ella was on one of the checkouts. She still lived at home on a farm in Lethen, near Nairn, eighteen miles away, but the nights she worked in Safeways she stayed with her auntie in Inverness. Sometimes on those nights she and Davy would finish work at the same time. Eventually, they decided to go for a drink together. Ella said just one because of college the next day. She also told Davy she had a boyfriend in Nairn. Davy said that was fine. So from then on they would often go for a drink after work and sometimes, especially at the end of the week, if they had no college the next day, they would drink more than one drink and then they would talk for a long time.

The place that Davy and Ella went for that first drink

together, and always from then on, was MacArthur's. It was Davy's choice. He told Ella that the original MacArthur, Old MacArthur, had come, like Davy himself, from Waternish. But this Old MacArthur had come a long time ago. Nowadays the bar was managed by his grandson. The old original MacArthur however, was still there, always sitting in the same corner with a gang of Skyemen. Bodaich (Old men). Davy told Ella (in a low voice) that Old MacArthur had been in school with Davy's father's father but that Old MacArthur had been, as a very young man, involved in a deep scandal and had had to leave Waternish and the Island. He had come to Inverness where he had prospered (as did all sinners in Inverness, according to Davy's Auntie Morag, who was not actually his auntie at all but his fifth cousin). Since then all, or most, of the people who came from Waternish to Inverness, even some of the most Godly, had been obliged to call in on Old MacArthur, as Davy had, when they first arrived in the city. Perhaps it was believed in Waternish that knowing Old MacArthur in a wicked place like Inverness was some kind of insurance, although no-one could have said exactly against what. Perhaps it was enough that nervous, new, or at least canny visitors from Waternish believed that no matter how wicked Inverness turned out to be, and there is no doubt there is wickedness in Inverness even to this day, Old MacArthur was a match for it, and he, if not on your side in virtue, still had some alliance with you geographically and this might give you some protection if it were ever to come to the bit, whatever that bit might be.

But Davy had never seen Old MacArthur as wicked in any way. To Davy he was just an old man who could, if anything, out-talk even Ella and who was, (old MacArthur himself had told this to Davy) and had always been, desperately homesick for Waternish and who would, later in the evenings, weep for his dead mother. Davy's Auntie (or fifth cousin) Morag said to Davy that Old MacArthur's mother had died of a broken heart, broken because of the scandal Old MacArthur had caused in his youth. But Davy's father said that the old woman had died of an ordinary heart attack, that heart attacks were the usual way for MacArthurs to go (and Old MacArthur's mother had been a MacArthur before she had married as well as after), and at an age when she would, as a woman on the islands, have been statistically expected to die at and this many years after her son's scandal. (The MacArthur men, however, tended to die much younger than the average for men, being afflicted by a tendency towards drink, dreaming and car crashing which often meant they did not get a chance to die of heart attacks. In fact it could be said that Old MacArthur's longevity was due to that old scandal having removed him from Waternish and those possibilities to, instead, homesickness and financial success in Inverness).

On one of those nights that they spent longer than usual in MacArthur's, Davy told Ella, when there was just the two of them at the table, that he had, so far, lived a useless life of no purpose and that he was not very sure that even this college course was the right thing for him to be doing. He said that, a year before, his sister-in -law, Cathie, a great organiser they said of her in Waternish, (while hiding out, or honing their excuses if they saw her coming their way) had volunteered him, while he was otherwise happily unemployed, as a driver on the old folk's minibus to Portree. While doing this he had had the vague idea that he might like to be, sometime, not necessarily soon, an ambulance driver. He had mentioned this to his sister-in-law during an awkward silence and the next thing he knew he was in Inverness on this course having been backed into it like a sheep into a pen. Now that he was here, he told Ella, there seemed to be more folk on the course, almost all females, aiming to be nurses than there were ambulance drivers.

"Well," said Ella, "there is nothing wrong with being a nurse. Except maybe the blood. My grandmother was a nurse most of her life and she said it is a great thing to be. She said men make good nurses. I wish you could have met her."

Ella got out her lipstick, already layers thick, (it seemed to Davy), but dissolved in places by the Guinness. It was Friday night. No college the next day. The renovation, Davy knew, was a sure sign that Ella was about to talk for a long time.

"Actually," she said. "I'm going to tell you a story about my grandmother the nurse. Only I know this story. It's a secret story. She told me before she died. It's a love story."

"Does it have a happy ending?" asked Davy, trying to speak lightly, but his heart had lurched towards his throat when Ella had said the word love.

"Of course not," said Ella. "What would be the point in that? In fact it has a very, very sad ending."

"Oh," he said.

"Right then," said Ella. "Here it is. My grandmother came to Nairnshire before the Second World War. She was twenty eight years old. She said that when she saw Nairnshire for the very first time she thought it was the most beautiful place she had ever seen. She said that when she stepped off the train she knew that she never wanted to live anywhere else ever again. And she never did. It was in Nairnshire, in Lethen where I live, that she met my grandfather. He was a farmer. His mother was bedridden and my grandmother, the district nurse, came up to the farm to attend to her. My grandfather fell in love with my grandmother straight away. So she said. After a time he asked her out and she said yes and then a time after that he asked her to marry him. The war was on by then and although, being a farmer, he did not have to go away and fight, there was a sense of urgency all around. He was not a great looking man, said my grandmother, but he was good fun so she said yes.

Now, in the time between when she had first come to Nairn and the time she was to marry my grandfather, about three years, my grandmother had often worked with a minister called John Forsythe. For example if someone had died, or was dying, or for all sorts of other reasons John Forsythe and my grandmother would have to work together. John Forsythe lived with his mother and his sister. Every Sunday my grandmother went to his church. Also her own father had been a minister so, having been brought up in the manse, in that sort of life, it meant she was very understanding, very sympathetic to some of the situations that a minister finds himself in.

Anyway, the night before my grandmother was due to get married, her landlady (my grandmother lived in the nurse's lodgings down by the river) came up to her room to tell her that the minister, John Forsythe, was here to see her. It was John Forsythe who was going to do the wedding ceremony the next afternoon so my grandmother thought it must be some detail about that, although she had seen him already earlier that day. She went down to the sitting room. The landlady brought them a cup of tea then left them alone.

As soon as she saw John Forsythe, even before the landlady had left the room, my grandmother could see that he was in a bit of a state. He was shaking and sweating. Even after the landlady had gone he did not speak. My grandmother tried to make conversation but for a long time, or maybe it just seemed like a long time, he said nothing.

Then suddenly he said, "Rachel. You cannot marry that James Ross. He is no good for you. He is not right for you. I am the right person for you. The person you should be with. Not him. I love you. I want you to marry me. Don't marry him. Do not make this mistake. I'm the one you should be marrying."

My grandmother was very shocked. She had never suspected anything like this. There had been no indication or warning from John Forsythe before. And there were all these folk already in Nairn who had travelled all the way, and not easily because of the war, for the wedding: Her two brothers, just off the convoys; her parents; her sister, other nurses and two old school friends. Also her work and her whole life here were now already completely interwoven into the lives of the farming families of Nairnshire and the family of my grandfather. There was no way she could back out now and still stay in Nairnshire.

And until that moment she had never thought of the minister John Forsythe as anything other than a good working acquaintance though it was true that he was very good looking and was often brought presents, cakes and biscuits mainly, by single women, and even married women, my grandmother said, of his congregation although these women must have known that his sister and mother baked enough for him already. My grandmother said, also, that he was a wonderful preacher with a lovely voice.

But my grandmother loved my grandfather, was sure that she did. Even with his reputation she was confident that he would settle down once they were married. She did worry about being a farmer's wife. She knew it would be hard. But she wanted to be with my grandfather, James Ross. She wanted to do her best. But now she was completely rattled. Confused. She felt things falling apart. More than ever she wanted to be married as if that would pull things back together.

But outwardly she stayed completely calm. She told John Forsythe she would not call off the wedding: That she was going to get married the next day. She told John Forsythe that she had appreciated working with him, and the friendship of himself and his mother and his sister, but that she was going to marry James Ross.

So eighteen hours later she did. And it was John Forsythe that did the job. He seemed relaxed and warm throughout the ceremony and spoke well, as usual. Afterwards people said it was a great service, great wedding, especially for wartime, better than many a more lavish affair in peacetime.

Four months later John Forsythe left Nairnshire and took another parish in Cromarty, over on the Black Isle. My grandmother did not see him or speak to him again for fifteen years, not until my grandfather, a wild man all his life, forgot a corner near the Cawdor Bridge and went through the dry-stone dyke at eighty miles an hour, across a field of nearly ready barley and, at the other side, down a forty foot bank into a deep pool on the River Nairn. People in Lethen said that my grandfather, having survived so many crashes in the past, had to be killed twice just to be sure: Once from the considerable crashing injuries and once more from the drowning.

Seven days after the funeral John Forsythe came over from the Black Isle to visit my grandmother. They drank tea together and John Forsythe said he would come back in a month to visit her again. That night, when he got home, he died of a heart attack. He was forty nine years old. So that was it. My grandmother never married again."

"God," said Davy, "that is a very, very sad story."

"Well," said Ella. "It's true the story itself is sad, but my grandmother herself sounded cheery enough, even while she was telling me the story."

"Right," said Davy.

So for the first two terms at the college Ella and Davy kept working at Safeways, meeting two or three nights a week, sometimes drinking too much, always talking.

During some of this time Davy had a girlfriend, kind of, and Ella had her boyfriend, Ian. But because Ella's main social life was at home in Nairnshire, Davy only met this Ian twice. The first time was when Ian came to pick up Ella from college and the second time when Davy went to Ella's nineteenth birthday party on the farm in Lethen. Afterwards he told Ella that he had enjoyed the party. In fact he had been very awkward with all these people who had known each other since they were children.

But Ella knew that he had not enjoyed himself and said she thought he'd been fed up. No, no, he said, he hadn't. He'd had a really good time.

"And you looked great," he said.

"Huh," she said. Then, "Did you like my green boots?"

He had.

By the third term, because of all the exams and projects, Ella and Davy had less and less time. They gave up their jobs at

Safeways altogether to concentrate on their college work. Eventually they hardly saw each other at all, only briefly in the corridors and doorways of the college and then they were usually with other folk, rushing about. By July Davy was back in Waternish for the summer, working in a hotel. Ella was home in Lethen on the farm. They had never managed a meeting to say goodbye.

Four years later Davy graduates as a nurse in Edinburgh. He gets the chance of a job back up North in Skye. Before he is due to start work he goes over to Glasgow to see his brother Dan.

Davy arrives in Glasgow at Queen Street Station. He catches the 41 bus to Drumchapel like Dan had told him to. He sits downstairs at the back of the bus. The bus stops at Hope Street. Ella comes down the stairs in a hurry from the upper deck and jumps off just as the door closes. Her hair is dark brown now with streaks of light green and gold. Davy jumps up but the bus is already moving. He cannot see Ella anymore. He gets off at the next stop and runs back along Hope Street. He still cannot see her. He runs up Renfrew Street where he knows the Art School is. He sees Ella ahead, her dancing walk.

He catches up with her.

"Ella," he says.

She stops, turns, "Davy. Davy. It's you."

"Ella," he says, "How are you?"

"Davy," she says, "Oh Davy, it's so good to see you. How are you?"

"I'm fine. Just fine," he says. "I'm a nurse now. Qualified. Finished. The real thing. I've got a job back up in Skye. In two weeks."

"Good for you, Davy. That's really good." she says. "I'm still a student. For another year. I hope. How long are you here for? Oh, it's great to see you again. It's really great."

So they are standing there on Renfrew Street, but it is like they were in MacArthur's again, talking, both at the same time, all the news, straightaway. And it's raining now (which they will remember later) but they hardly notice with so much to say.

And Davy asks, "How is Ian?"

"Oh that was a long time ago." Ella laughs. "I'm sure he is fine. I was at his wedding not long ago."

"Look," she says, "I've only to collect a couple of things from the art school and then I've got to go back to the flat, it's not that far, and cook a meal for some folk. And I'm a bit late already. So why don't you come as well. Then we can talk."

Davy knows he can phone his brother Dan, who will not be bothered by the change of plan (if he even remembers there was one). But he also knows that, when he and Ella start to walk, go to collect whatever she needs to collect, then to her flat, and then the cooking, and next will be the other folk arriving (if they are not already there), there will be no chance to say what he needs to say, what he has needed to say for so long. And even after all her visitors have gone, even if he does manage to say these things, she might think it is just the drink, for there is sure to be drink, or she herself will be a bit drunk, or she might be tired by the time they are alone, or there might be no chance to be alone, and it might be too late anyway: It could go all wrong.

He knows that if he is going to say anything at all it must be now. And it is best while they are both still sober.

So he says, "Ella, I want to tell you that I love you and it's been for a very long time, probably since the first moment I ever saw you and although everything in my life is just fine now, also nothing is unless it is to be with you. I want to be with you always, not every minute of the day I mean, but for our lives. What I mean is I'd like us to be together, maybe get married if you'd like, have children or things like that, live back up North, only if you wanted. I mean if that's not what you want I'll be ok. I mean I'll never love anyone else, or ever have since first I saw you, or ever will again, except you. I mean I'll be fine, only I love you and I always will."

Ella smiles. The gaps between her teeth that she always told him were much healthier than teeth close together and the dimple in her left cheek that her mother told Davy at Ella's nineteenth birthday party was not a dimple at all but the scar from the time she fell off her bike when she was five years old and the brake lever went through her cheek.

And Davy knows now for sure how glad he is that he became a nurse. It means that from now on he'll always be ready. Whatever happens. He'll do extra time in accident and emergency, in intensive care. Extra training. He'll be ready. He'll get to know the very best doctors, the best specialists of everything that could ever happen to Ella. From now on he'll be with her. He'll know what to do.

And Ella is still smiling. She has put her hands to her face.

So Davy tells her he knows about falling in love. But he says this is more than falling in love. It is more like ever since he first met her, love has been falling into him. Like he had been empty and bit by bit he has been filled by loving her all this time.

And by now he has told her how much he loves her until he has run out of breath, run out of words. (This is only temporary, he has been storing speeches to Ella, millions of words now, for five years). And she is looking at him, her smile and dimpled cheek already mentioned, her eyes bright, and different colours, which he had never noticed before, not in Inverness, it must be the Glasgow light that folk talk about, or maybe the position, the tilt of her head. He is afraid now, having stopped talking, in the silence, of what she might say.

And up and down Renfrew Street the Glasgow people are passing by, giving a glance now and then, or more, as they proceed, their famous keen eye for style, at Ella's clothes, ignoring Davy.

"Ok then," she says, "Davy. That all sounds like a right fine plan to me. I think we should get started straight away."

Then she gives him a doubtful look. "The only thing I'm wondering is, be honest, are you not a bit worried about our children's noses? I mean, the combination."

"Oh, no, no, no, not at all, Ella," he says. "No. I'm not. They'll be great. Great noses. The best. Honestly. Trust me. I guarantee it. Absolutely guaranteed great noses."

"Well, that's it then," Ella says. "Decided."

Many years later, but while they are still young, Ella and Davy are driving from the Raigmore Hospital in Inverness, home to Waternish. On these long days that they go to Inverness for Davy's treatment they could stay overnight in Inverness, or with Ella's folks in Lethen, but lately Davy always likes to get back to Waternish.

"I don't fancy dying in Inverness," he says.

"Well, your old pal Old MacArthur did," says Ella.

"Aye, and they had to carry him all the way home to Waternish to bury. I'd prefer, and I'm sure he would have too, to see the road and the hills on that last journey across."

But the chemotherapy has made him tired and sick so by the time they get to Kintail he is sleeping and by the time they cross to the island it is night. In Waternish their children will be in their beds already in Davy's sister's house. And above the dark road ahead Ella can see the heather fires still glowing on the hills. Inside the car she can smell the peat smoke from the burning. And she can see that Davy's face (that in daytime is bleached, the skin shrunk over the bone) is now, in the reds and yellows of the dashboard lights, looking healthy again, young like the boy she first saw seeing her in the corridors of the Inverness Midmills College.

And by the time she turns the car at the Fairy Bridge, off the Dunvegan Road, towards Waternish, Davy is waking again.

"130 miles down, four to go," she says. "We'll soon be home."

"Ella," he says.

And sometimes it is almost too difficult for her to speak.

"I know, Davy, I know."

"I think that'll be the last trip to Inverness, Ella" he says. "I don't want to leave Waternish again."

"I know," she says. "I know."

And on Sunday she will drive him again to the church of his parents, and of their parents, and of theirs before that, where, two years before, for the first time in her life, Ella had heard a congregation sing in the old way, the precentor calling out the lines of the psalm and the worshippers then joining his lead, the sound gathering, advancing slowly, steadily, their voices separating and uniting until they had risen together to such a beauty that it had nearly broken open Ella's contained heart, had carried her shaken and awed upwards, and upwards, until she was falling then with the sound as it settled to almost a silence but out of which the precentor's voice alone again proceeded, and then the congregation, in the fullness of all their voices, and Davy with them.

"I didn't know you could sing, Davy," Ella had said after that first service.

"Well," he'd said, "No. I didn't used to be able to. Maybe it's some kind of side effect of dying."

Then he'd laughed, (Ella being a truly terrible, though optimistic, singer), "Something for you to look forward to, Ella."

"Bloody cheek," she'd retaliated, "And I was just being kind. Your singing is still pretty bad."

And after the service they will drive down to the edge of the sea where Davy will sit and watch Ella walking on the stones in her dark Sabbath clothes.

Two years before, when Davy had first told Ella that he would like to go again to the services of his childhood, she had told him that she would like to go with him. He had said then, looking at her pinks and purples, her cherry lipstick, her bracelets and glitter galore, that people usually (he meant always) dressed very plainly and quietly for the services (and most for the other six days of the week as well, though he did not say that either). Ella had said that this was no bother to her, the dresser-upper since birth. Davy then said that that was good. It was just that he'd wondered whether a highly decorated person like herself...... So Ella had asked did he doubt that she could manage to dress appropriately for the occasion? No, no, he'd said. No, he didn't. So she'd asked, "Is it that you don't want me to go? That you want to go by yourself?"

"Oh no," he'd said. "No. Definitely not. I want you to come too. It's great if you do. Really great. Better. Much better."

"Ok then," she'd said, and on that first Sunday that they were to go together she had appeared, after hours of preparation, having got up early, in a dark floppy bonnet, (over even her ears; it was a cold rainy day), a black and dark gray Victorian dress with jet buttons, dark stockings and black lace up boots (that had once been green). Davy had laughed then at his own reaction, the surge of life and happiness through his body when he saw her, her beauty, and he'd known again that, even in this great effort that she had made at humility and drabness, there was something in Ella that could not be disguised, that no camouflage could ever suppress. He knew then, as he knows now, that he would have been dead already, long before, the disease having got the better of him, only that she was there, with him, and that one sight of her, always, even one thought of her, made his blood flow richer and faster, his heart beat so strongly again that he believes that he might live forever in his love for her.

Tonight, down ahead, nearly home, they can see the light left on for them by Davy's sister.

"Davy," Ella says again. Then she speaks to him in Gaelic. And this is another thing about her. All the years that they have lived here and that she has grappled, in her energetic and haphazard way, with this language, which she will speak whenever possible, before anything else, at any opportunity, in her haywire grammar and high North East accents, her wild hybrid approximations that have so often baffled her listeners and made Davy love her even more.

"No, no, it's Gaelic, right enough," he would tell her, "and something else as well."

But the words that she speaks tonight as she slows the car in the darkness and turns onto their road are the first that she had ever learned in Gaelic, long ago, from Davy, and so have been practiced all their lives together, have been so often said that they are fluent now with time and use.

"O, Davy, Davy, a ghraidh, 's tu gaol mo chridhe." ("Oh, Davy, Davy, my darling, you are the love of my heart.")

Not broken, like these same words will be in that morning not very long from now, by grief and desolation, at the graveside high above the sea when she and the children, and so many people that they are spilled beyond the walls out onto the fields, lay Davy down into the earth.

And in that morning, to the hills and the grass and the sky, to the rocks and the islands and the sea, and to the sheep grazing, and to the hands of her children warm in her hands, to the salt in her mouth, and the crofts in the distance and the cows and the crows and the seabirds and their sounds, to the mourners moving towards their cars, and the narrowness of the road down, to the cold wind and to her skin, to the blood in her veins, and to the stillness of time in that time in that room after Davy's breathing had stopped, and to her waiting by his side till long after darkness for his next breath that never came. And to her turning now from his grave to follow the others, and the stone of the path on which she walks away, she whispers,

"O gaol mo chridhe, Chan'eil fios agam ciamar a bhios mi beo anns an t-saoghal tha seo as d'aonais." ("Oh love of my heart, I do not know how to go on living in this world without you.")

Linda And The French Hordes

There was a time, in 1966, the summer after her mother had died, that Linda believed the whole of the West Coast had been invaded by young Frenchmen. Every hotel she worked in had at least one. Sometimes two. Sometimes even three.

Linda had left Nairn in spring and was moving around a lot that year, restless, but eventually she came to spend the last of the summer season near Gairloch in a hotel run by two women who the locals and hotel staff (which was half the locals) called the G and T.

The G and T, Mrs Grant and Miss Thomas, had first met in the army during the Second World War where, amongst their many other successes, they had managed to keep the pregnancy rate of their girls (as they called them) well below the military average, leaving the girls free to go out and fight the good fight. When the war was over the G and T had come to Gairloch to cook the best food North of anywhere and South of everywhere else. They had tried to run the hotel on military lines but this efficiency was continuously sabotaged by their tendency to a deep kindness that they could never quite suppress. They suited Linda well. And even if there had not been French Jack, the waiter, who was also there for the season, she would have stayed.

Linda probably did not fall in love with Jack straightaway. Not until she heard him speak. But then she certainly did, at least with his voice, his language. And Jack never spoke English unless he had to. And when he did, or had what he had said translated, it was always a great disappointment to Linda. Once, early in their relationship, as they lay in her bunk in the chalet at the back of the hotel on a night that had never got dark, she had asked him to tell her what he had been murmuring to her at great length for hours, sending a helpless liquidity up and down her bones and her flesh to runny honey, and he had tried to translate what he had been saying which, approximately, had been about his difficulties in getting to a toilet whenever he had been hitch-hiking in Britain and that once, desperate, he had had to go in the middle of a traffic island in Dundee, his head (tete) poking out of the shrubbery (bosquet) watching the clockwise (dans le sans aiguilles d'une montre) afternoon (apres-midi) traffic (trafic).

After this Linda accepted that what she loved about him was the music of his language and the lazy, slow motion, stopping-for-a-coffee-break-now-and-then nature of his love making. These things were more than enough, she reckoned, for the duration.

Physically, although he had extraordinary vanity and self-confidence, Jack was as ugly a man as you could find. He was lumpy and awkward with springy and unstyleable blond hair, big ears, big nose, wonky teeth. He staggered and flopped about like a man on a rough sea, terrifying the customers he waited dangerously and dramatically upon. He looked badly put together, his chest like a loose sack of sticks, spindly legs, hopeless bony knees. All his elegance was in his voice. When Jack spoke waves of weakness and birdsong went through Linda like strong drink. She felt airy and weightless like she had earlier that year in Oban, recovering from flu. When he spoke Linda felt shaky, dizzy, helpless, her heart battering like a prisoner inside her chest. When Jack spoke Linda's clothes took themselves off and threw themselves around the room.

Then the season was nearly over. With only two weeks to go before Jack left, Linda knew she was pregnant. But she hardly considered telling him. She decided they would enjoy the rest of their time together. The day before she saw him for the last time ever, they climbed the hills to the old houses that had been destroyed in the clearances and sat in the sun on the near buried stones. Linda knew Jack would go home and probably never think of her again, unless, in his middle age, and like those Italian or German ex-prisoners of war who sometimes returned to Nairn, he was afflicted by that sense of loss that took those ageing Italians and Germans back to Scotland to look for the local girls who they had loved once, who had been their youth.

But Linda's father, her Italian father, had never come back. He might have thought sometimes about her mother, and even wondered about Linda, who he had known about, who had been born before he left, but who he had never seen. Her father, from her mother's description of him, had been a gentle and attentive man and it seemed to Linda that he was, perhaps, the sort of man who would remember.

Or maybe not. Linda also now suspected that he and her mother might have had the same difficulties of understanding as she and Jack had had and this, combined with the situation during the war, the secrecy of consorting with the enemy (Linda prefers cavorting with the enemy), might mean that what her mother had imagined her Italian was like might have been very different from the truth.

With Jack gone Linda stayed on with the G and T. The hotel was quieter now but there was enough to do. Eventually Linda told them she was going to have a baby. She expected to have to leave, but the G and T reacted to the whole situation with extraordinary enthusiasm. They installed Linda in the annexe cottage and flooded her with attention and warmth (coal fires roaring all winter and spring and into the summer). Polly (called after a lost relative of Mrs Grant's) was born in May. Linda and Polly lived on with Mrs Grant and Miss Thomas (they all kept up some pretence of Linda's independence; separate quarters; exchange of work for rent, but in reality any sense of reckoning had been lost early in their happiness together) until Polly was seven when, very suddenly, Mrs Grant died.

Miss Thomas and Linda worked hard, kept the hotel going,

successfully, for the next year. They needed the task. But eventually Miss Thomas knew she could not settle in the absence of Mrs Grant in the place they had tried so hard to make together. She decided she would like to travel again which she had not much since before the war. She would go first to Australia to see her brother. The hotel was sold. Linda and Polly went to Nairn, Linda to work as an auxillary in the Nairn Town and County Hospital, maybe eventually to be a nurse. She felt, at twenty eight years old, ready to study and learn, which she had never felt before.

Linda is still living in Nairn twenty years later. Of course, during this time, which is, after all, seven thousand three hundred and five days, Linda has had many adventures. Mostly not the kind that get into the newspapers or on television, just the real, ordinary, good and bad kind that go on for us all, although part of one of Linda's adventures did get reported in the Press and Journal, the Inverness Courier and in the Nairnshire, and for nine seconds on the Grampian news: It was played down a bit in case it discouraged tourists in an already poor season. What happened was, in 1978, in Inverness, Linda was mugged by a very incompetent mugger. The mugging itself had been competent enough: He had knocked Linda to the ground and snatched her bag. But as he ran away across The Ness Bridge he was struck by a Triumph Trident motor bike. Later the bike rider told Linda he and the mugger had been in school together. The mugger survived this running down well enough, but as he rose from the ground and tried to limp away he was hit by a mini-bus which was arriving from Dingwall with nine large adult shoppers on their way to Marks and Spencers. Linda felt somehow responsible for the carnage and visited the mugger, a nineteen year old called John Taylor, in Raigmore hospital. John Taylor wept heart breakingly on Linda's arm and said he was sorry. He said he had decided to change his ways: No more drugs. Nowadays he is married and works for the Hydro-Board in Skye as a linesman. Every time he has a new son he sends Linda a postcard. The postcards arrive nine months or so after he and his wife Julia (she is a bit older, an ex-hippie child who had arrived in the District of Waternish in the sixties with a rock star's retinue) try for a daughter. There have been eight postcards so far. Linda tries to suppress the only occasional worry that the boys will grow up to be as wild as their father was in his youth and that the population of Waternish is in for a bit of a fracas sometime in the future. So far she has found the boys to be very sweet and gentle (like their mother).

Linda also went to Australia three times in the twenty years. Once for four months which she spent with Miss Thomas, drunk on red wine and travelling across desert places in Miss Thomas' old car. They made a pilgrimage to Alice Springs in honour of their favourite book of the Gairloch days. In Alice Springs they met many people willing to supply them with even more red wine. Also in the twenty years Linda has had two very unsuccessful relationships. One with a gentle, poetic and hopeless drunkard and one with a drunkard who was not gentle or poetic at all. There was also a long lasting situation which may or may not have been a relationship. Linda still doesn't know. She has never had any more children after Polly but she was left with Polly's cat when Polly left home. Linda never before had much time for cats but sometimes, lately, she finds herself talking about her day to this cat, Hamie. She is less disturbed now than she was when she first noticed herself doing this. She reckons if there is to be a male creature in her house, Hamie is as good as you can get. At the very least he listens to everything Linda has to say.

So Linda still lives in Nairn. She is a District Nurse. Polly has been somewhere near Birmingham for six months. Before Birmingham she was near London. Before London, near somewhere else.

In September, 1998, Linda finds a lump in her left breast.

She writes to Polly.

"I am sorry you never had a father," she says.

Polly writes back, "I did have a father. Only I never met him. But I had you and the G and T. Then you and I went to live in Nairn and I had that bedroom with the sloping roof, remember? And at night I could hear the rain and wind and I would shut my eyes and travel away out across the darkness, across the world, to my father in France, and he would be playing cards, laughing and drinking with his friends, and I would go up to him and I would say, see, I am your daughter, Polly. And he would be astonished. He would drop his cards. He would rise from his seat, crying with happiness, shouting to his friends, look, look, and he would fall to his knees saying, this is my daughter, this is my daughter, oh this is my daughter, holding me, holding me. Or sometimes, by the time I came to France he would be dead. And I would walk to the graveyard in the rain alone, carrying the flowers, and walk along the paths till I found his name and there it would be, written in the wet stone, 'Jack, father of Polly'. Then I would lay the flowers on his grave and walk away.

And those nights I travelled like that to see him were all I ever needed from him. That I could find him so easily whenever I wanted.

Instead of a father and mother I had you. Would a separate father have helped me dye my hair pink? Would he have bathed my septic ears when I had tried to pierce them myself? Would he have put cream on the slashes on my arms or held me and cried when no one ever asked me out anywhere? Could I have screamed at him, thrown glasses and dishes at him, been sick over him, kept him up all night? Maybe. I don't know. But did he wait for me for a thousand hours in hospitals and police stations? No. He didn't. You did. So there it is. I had you."

Polly heads North, home to Nairn, to be with Linda while she is dying. And Miss Thomas, bronzed and weeping, flies from Australia as soon as Polly phones her with the news.

Together they care for Linda.

At 3 o'clock in the afternoon on Sunday 23rd of August 2000 the last thing Linda sees in this world is Polly's face. Linda notices that Polly has taken out the studs in her lower lip, maybe for the occasion. Linda can no longer speak so she cannot ask. She hopes that there will be young men at her funeral. More choice for Polly. Cousins maybe, but nevertheless (Polly's blood has been freshened up enough by international relationships to stand a bit of inbreeding). Perhaps Polly could marry a farmer. At least then she would stay in one place, not wandering around everywhere like she's been doing so far. Linda can easily see Polly out there, squelching through the mud in wellies, carrying feed buckets, trailing babies and hens, tattoos rippling with the effort.

Lorraine And The Cockerel

When I was twelve my father, driving home drunk and fast from the Auction Mart in Inverness, drove underneath the back of a lorry which was parked at the Gollanfield crossroads.

It was said in Nairn afterwards that he was cut in half, as his car was. But my mother said he wasn't. She went to Nairn hospital that night to identify him and when she came home she told us he was dead alright, but intact. This was early December, the sixth, 1958. Five days later when we buried him, Christmas was just two weeks away.

There were five of us in our family. Thousands if you count all the relatives but here I mean just my father, my mother, my brother Hugh, (the son and heir; to the name if nothing else), and Mary Ann who was the baby. And me, Lorraine. I was twelve, Hugh was ten and Mary Ann was four.

My father was a sheep dealer. My mother stayed at home. Moaning at me. If you combine sheep dealing with drinking like my father did there is never much money in the bank. So this Christmas with him dead and gone looked bleak. And we usually had very lavish Christmases. Not a lot in the way of presents but plenty food and drink. In fact we ate well all the time and I never considered ourselves poor. My mother did. This Christmas it looked like she might be right. There were always my father's four brothers and three sisters but my mother was not about to ask them for help. She was a Church of Scotland Minister's daughter, a daughter of the Manse. She might accept help if any of them thought of offering it. She would not ask. Not even my Uncle Thomas.

Uncle Thomas was my father's oldest brother. He was born in 1898 and he had flown during the First World War over France. Fighting. When he came home in 1919 to my grandfather's farm he fell in love with a girl called Sheila

Munro. He wanted to marry her but she said no. My mother always told me this with satisfaction. She considered this Sheila Munro had made a wise move. My mother often said of herself that there were only two mistakes in her life. The first was marrying my father. The second was having children.

"But you'll never have those problems, Lorraine," she said. "You have never been a beauty. You'll have to be a nurse or something, get your own house. There will not be men queuing up to take care of you."

My uncle Thomas's heart was broken. He went to India and never married. In 1948 my Grandfather died and Uncle Thomas, the oldest son, came home and took over the farm.

A week after my own father's funeral, with one week to go till Christmas, Uncle Thomas phoned my mother. He had always been shy of women, especially my mother. Her smoking and talking and conclusions frightened him. He mumbled and stammered on the phone but my mother understood that he would bring us down a bird for our Christmas table.

"So that's one relief," said my mother. "With potatoes and vegetables, maybe a trifle. Cake. And there is still a bit of drink left through the room from the funeral. For visitors. It'll be plenty."

The night before Christmas Eve Uncle Thomas arrived. My mother was out of the house, just for a minute. He gave me and Hugh and Mary Ann an envelope each. As soon as he was gone we opened them up. I got a Boot's token for five shillings and so did Hugh and Mary Ann. Uncle Thomas would not come in. He was shy of children as well as women.

"Lorraine," he said, very red in the face and leaning on the door (he had carried up a full bag of King Edwards). "That's just a few tatties I've put in the back of the shed for your mother. The bird is in the boot of the car. Come on down to the gate and get it."

At the car he lifted out of the boot a squawking, pecking, kicking sack.

"It's a cockerel," he said. "He's a fair size. There will be plenty eating there for you all. I'll have to rush. Tell your Mother a Happy Christmas from me."

He drove off.

I could hardly get the bag up to the house. If I tried to lift it the weight swung against me and the creature pecked and scratched me through the sacking. I had always loved my Uncle Thomas, but not at that moment.

"God. God. God," said my mother when she came home. The sack was kicking its way round the kitchen. "Trust him. Well Lorraine, you'll just have to take it down to Jimmy's in the morning. Ask him to kill it and pluck it for us. Put it in the shed for the night."

The next morning the beast was crowing and making a terrible racket though still inside the bag. It was unusual said my mother, they usually went quiet in darkness. But he had pecked so many holes in the sacking it was probably quite bright in there.

I set off down the town trying to avoid any injuries from the furious bird. Hugh and Mary Ann were away to Boots already. Across the road, brushing down her steps, was Mrs MacAskill, watching me.

"What have you got there, Lorraine?" she shouted. So I went over. There was never any getting past Mrs MacAskill anyway.

"It's a cockerel we got from my Uncle Thomas for our Christmas dinner but he's still alive so I'm taking him down to Jimmy's," I said.

"Well now. Here. Let's have a look at him," said Mrs MacAskill. Mrs MacAskill kept hens in her back garden. I put the bag down and opened the top a bit.

"Right down," said Mrs MacAskill. "Let him out. Let's get a right good look at the man."

I pulled the bag right down and let him and Mrs MacAskill see each other. He went very quiet and still. Subdued. Mrs MacAskill had buried two farmer husbands and she knew no fear of any male creature that I had ever heard of.

"Well," she said. "Well. You really are a fine fellow, aren't you? So why is Thomas giving you the death sentence then? What have you been up to?"

"I'll tell you what, Lorraine," she said. "You go and tell your mother that I'll give her two fat hens for this lad here. They are all plucked and ready now. It's not been the same out the back since the old one died and this rascal would cheer things up quite a bit I'm sure."

"No," I said, glad and relieved. "No, I'll not need to ask. It'll be fine with her. That would be just great Mrs MacAskill."

"Right then. Good." said Mrs MacAskill. "Come on in and we'll just get them now."

"And you, my lad," she said to the cockerel. "In this gate here with me. This is home."

In 1983 my Uncle Thomas died. He had retired from the farm and gone to live near the sea. I was away from Nairn and had been for a long time. I came home for his funeral. His last ten years he had spent fishing and shooting with his pals. Or so we had thought.

At his funeral my second cousin, whose father was Uncle Thomas's lawyer, told me and my mother that Uncle Thomas had left all his money and his house to an auctioneer's widow who lived in Carrbridge.

"Huh! Some shy of women after all, your Uncle Thomas," said my mother who had had three, or maybe more, large whiskies already. "And it must be over thirty miles to Carrbridge."

But she was satisfied with the bad news. It was true to her in a way that money had never been.

I don't know how long the cockerel, Mrs MacAskill's fellow, lived. Certainly he was still alive in 1962 when I left home. I was sixteen. It was June. Summer. Very early in the morning, bright and fresh. I went out the back door of our house and down the side, walking on the grass and not on the gravel.

The cockerel was outside Mrs MacAskill's house on the pavement where, each day, he waited to attack passing collies and cairn terriers. He was watching me as I walked down the road with my bag on my shoulder.

At the far end, before I turned the corner to the station, I looked back. He was still there, watching, standing in the sunshine, the shadows crossing Nairn eastwards and, between us, the empty road.

Lorraine And The Night Bob Gillies Went To See Allan Munro

In all the fourteen years my mother and father were together, every Tuesday that my father went to Inverness Auction Mart he got drunk. When he came home he would cause havoc. My mother tried various ways to stop this happening but by the time I was ten she had given up hoping that she could stop him drinking. All her plans were concentrated on changing the wild things he usually did when he was drunk. One of these plans was Allan Munro, my father's friend.

Allan Munro was known to be not a drinker. This did not mean that Allan Munro did not drink at all. Rather it meant that when he drank, although he could be just as drunk as the rest of them, he remained fairly benign, not looking for trouble and destruction. My mother believed, hoped, temporarily, that if my father went to the Mart with Allan Munro then my father would return home the same happy and easy going, though drunk, kind of person as Allan.

So it was that on Tuesdays, for several weeks, Allan Munro would drive over from his place to ours and collect my father and together they would go to Inverness where they would buy and sell animals and drink. It was on one of these Tuesdays that, taking a break from the auction ring, they went over to the Plough Bar across the street. They were still there when Bob Gillies came in and the three of them then drank together.

Eventually, more than a while later, Allan and my father went back to the Mart and left Bob Gillies in the Plough.

It was already late afternoon and dark when Allan Munro drove my father home and then drove home himself. Allan's farm, like most in Lethen, was without electricity. Allan came in out of the darkness towards the only light; the kitchen and his wife Margaret.

After his tea Allan said to Margaret, "God. I'm tired, Meg. I think I'll off up to my bed. I've got an early start tomorrow with the lorry coming."

"All right Allan," Margaret said. "You do that. I've just a bit of baking to do then I'll be up."

A while later, with the Tilley lamp burning bright and hissing, Margaret was making the scones when there was a wild hammering at the back door. She went out with the lamp and there, against the night, stood Bob Gillies with his twelve bore shotgun held across his chest.

"Where is Allan?" said Bob Gillies, with no hello to Margaret.

"Good God, Bob," said Margaret. "Is that you? Allan's gone off up the hill to see Old Grant. He'll not be back for a while yet."

"I'll wait for him," said Bob.

"Come in then, come in." Margaret held wide the door. "I'll make some tea and you'll taste a scone."

Bob Gillies came in and stood first, but then sat in the kitchen. He kept his twelve bore ready across his knees. Margaret made the tea and buttered Bob three of the hot fresh scones. And jam.

At first Bob did not touch anything but Margaret said, "Come on, Bob, come on. Your tea will be cold! Drink up and try a scone."

So he did.

"And how is Elsie?" asked Margaret.

"Fine," said Bob Gillies.

"And how are the three boys? I've not seen them since ages."

"They're fine," he said again.

"Three boys are a terrible handful," said Margaret, hoping that Allan would not be wakened by the talk and appear at the kitchen door in his pyjamas.

"Aye," said Bob Gillies.

Margaret kept making scones, kept talking and after three hours Bob Gillies stood up.

"Thank you, Margaret," he said. "For the tea and scones. I doubt if I'll be seeing Allan tonight."

"Ah well," said Margaret, and the table fuller of baking than she would ever know what to do with.

Bob Gillies went out into the night. She heard him drive away.

Margaret Munro went up to the bedroom. The room was freezing cold but the bed was warm with Allan and the smell of the whisky. He stirred as she climbed in beside him.

"Bob Gillies has just been down," said Margaret. "He was here to shoot you."

"Good God," said Allan into the darkness. "Are you sure?"

The next Tuesday I did not go to school. I went to Inverness with Allan Munro and my father. This was not supposed to be a treat. It was the echo of an old failed plan of my mother's, the plan before Allan Munro. She had used to send me to Inverness with my father because she had believed he would not drink when he was with his oldest daughter. My mother was wrong. In fact, he was probably worse. He knew he could rely on me to find the car and put the key in the ignition for him.

Allan drove over and picked us up. I was in the back and my father in the front passenger seat. We went down to the main road. As we waited for a break in the traffic I could see the backs of my father's and Allan Munro's heads, balding, grey, silhouetted against the front windscreen. They were not old men. My father was about fifty and Allan maybe the same. But within two years, although at different times and places, and for different reasons, they would both be dead.

On the main road, we drove the two miles past Nairn to where the road ran in a five mile straight towards Inverness.

"God, Allan," said my father. "I hear Bob Gillies was going to shoot you last Tuesday night. What in God's name did he want to do that for?"

"God Knows," said Allan. "Maybe.....," but then he started to laugh.

He tried again to speak but every time he tried he started to laugh. Then my father started laughing with him. Allan kept saying "Maybe....," but that was always as far as he got and I started too although I had no idea what we were laughing at. By then Allan was laughing so much he could hardly keep the car on the road. He was shaking and blinded with tears and us all in pain in our stomachs. So he had to stop the car. He pulled up on the grass verge with us all crying and laughing and Allan still trying to speak but that only making us worse.

Eventually we began to calm down and only snorting occasionally or saying, "God, oh God, oh God," with the aching, and wiping the tears from our eyes till we were quiet and done with laughing.

And outside the haar was breaking thin across the fields, the sky over us yellow grey. And in the north towards the Firth the black crows were rising, the time still early, but it was never going to be any more light that day.

Allan started the car and we drove on towards Inverness.

Years later, in Aberdeen, Bob Gillies' son, Peter, and I met up and we went around together. One night, at his place, we were lying together in the dark, smoking, and I asked him if he knew why his father had tried to shoot Allan Munro.

But Peter was very angry. He said it had never happened. He said people in Nairn were always making up stories like that but none of it was true. I think until then we had both hoped that our being together would be something, perhaps some kind of happiness. I would have said, although I didn't, that I was in love with him. But after that night, after that question, things were never going to be any good and eventually, or perhaps it was even from that moment, we never saw each other again.

Lorraine In Edinburgh In The Cold

She wakes on the bus and steps off into the hard morning winter light. She walks dazzled towards the flats, crunching the snow and glass beneath her boots.

In the stair she climbs to the first floor. The third door is covered by an almost fresh plywood panel, already cigarette burned around and over the melted plastic spyhole. One name is written small on the wood in pencil. There is no bell.

She takes off her right glove and knocks on the door.

She waits for a while then she knocks again. She feels the silence from the flat enter the bones of her hand. She feels the cold walls gather about her, the frozen air from outside coming up the stair at her back.

Christmas Trees

Lorraine is in the bath in her mother's house in Nairn and her mother is hammering and shouting at the bathroom door. The water pouring out of the taps into the bath is making so much noise that Lorraine cannot hear what her mother is saying. The bathroom is freezing cold and Lorraine is under hot water up to her eyes. She does not want to move so she pays no heed.

Later Lorraine dresses and comes through to the front room where her mother is sitting with John and Robert, Lorraine's boys. John is ten and Robbie is six. Lorraine's mother is seventy-three years old. A year ago she broke her ankle and it has never healed properly. She can hardly walk. She has had cancer and two heart attacks.

Lorraine says, "What were you shouting?"

Her mother says, "I was going to tell you we either die from the feet up or the head down. Look at me. My mind is great, better than ever, but I can hardly creep about. Then look at her over the road. The same age. She could run a four minute mile but she cannot remember her own name."

"Well," says Lorraine, "We can also die from the middle outwards with peritonitis and other things."

"Oh, good God, Lorraine," says her mother, "Sometimes it's just not worth speaking to you. You strangle everything I say with your qualifications."

"I'm going to go down the town in a minute," says Lorraine. "Do you need anything? Were you wanting more cigarettes?"

It is the first day of their Christmas holiday in Nairn. Lorraine says to the boys, "What shall we do today?"

Robbie says, "We could go to the graveyard and see your daddy."

John says, "Or we could go to the river."

"Or both, we'll do both," says Lorraine.

Nairn graveyard is on a hill where the town ends and the farmlands begin. John, Robbie and Lorraine visit all the Ross graves. She reads the stones to the boys. There is her father, her uncles, her grandmother and grandfather. The great aunts. The boys walk along the wall where Lorraine's mother told them that the suicides were buried. They reach the stone of Lorraine's great grandfather and great grandmother. From here they can see to the hills and farms where they had worked. It is late in December, the wind is very cold but they stay a while.

Robbie asks, "Can they hear us?"

Lorraine says, "Yes, I think so. In a way."

"Do you say anything to them?"

"No. I just kind of listen."

Robbie listens. "I can't hear anything. What do you hear?"

Lorraine laughs. She kisses him. "I just hear my teeth chattering and the wind in the trees. It's time to go. What shall we do now?"

"I'm freezing cold Mammy," says John. "Let's go up the river."

In December, 1955, Lorraine is nine years old. It is late afternoon and already dark in the kitchen. Her mother has gone up to the cottages. Lorraine is waiting for her to come home to light the lamps. Through the kitchen window, Lorraine sees her father's car stop at the back gate. After a while the car door opens and her father falls out onto the ground. He manages up but he falls twice before he reaches the back porch. In the porch they keep the coats and the boots and his guns.

Her father comes through into the kitchen. He is carrying his gun. It is an old twelve bore double barrel shotgun with external hammers and engraving on the sides.

He says, "Go and get me some cartridges from the bag, Lorraine."

Lorraine goes to the porch and she takes two red and brass

cartridges from the bag hanging behind the door. She brings them to her father. He loads the cartridges in his gun.

He says, "Stand against the wall there, Lorraine. I am going to shoot you first."

Lorraine stands against the wall. Her father aims the gun at her head but he is very unsteady with the drink. He tries to steady the gun by resting the muzzle on the bridge of her nose but she is shaking so much that the metal is stotting up and down on the bone. She leans back and presses her head against the wall to hold still. She is worrying that her mother might arrive back from the cottages. If her mother were to walk in the kitchen now and see Lorraine's father shooting Lorraine she would not be pleased and Lorraine, with her head jammed between the wall and the gun, does not feel in the right position for the excitement. In the darkness she looks along the double barrels to her father's face. Sometimes when he is this drunk he goes into short sleeps. He will stand still and stay in the same position with his eyes closed for what seems like a long time. Perhaps it is only minutes. It is no good trying to sneak off because that always wakes him up. Lorraine is glad to see that he has not cocked back the two hammers on the gun so there is no chance he will shoot her by accident while he is asleep. She knows it is best not to move at all but in his sleep he is leaning forward on the gun and the metal edge has started to cut into her nose. It is too sore. She reaches up slowly to try to take some of the weight of him and the gun off her face. When she touches the barrels, he opens his eyes.

In the New Year of 1988, on the sixth of January, Lorraine, John and Robert leave Nairn very early in the morning. Lorraine's mother stands in her doorway. There are tears held back in her eyes. She leans on her stick. She watches them walk out into the darkness.

"Well Lorraine," she says, "You've made a right mess of life. And these two poor wee souls with no father to speak of."

Lorraine kisses her mother on the cheek, "Goodbye Mammy, and don't worry, it's alright. Everything is fine. Don't stand at the door. Go back in out of the cold. I'll phone you as soon as we are back in Edinburgh."

The sea mists and the darkness swirl around the streets as they walk to the station. Lorraine is following John and Robert. She feels the cold wind and her mother's love at her back.

The boys are running ahead and she cannot see them. She shouts into the mist, "Don't go too far ahead and don't cross any streets without me."

They are on the train and it is leaving Nairn station. They are looking out the window into darkness, into nothing.

She always knew her father would not shoot her. She knew he loved her and that, one day, when she grew up, they would sort things out together. She knew that one day there would be good things that would happen, that they would do together. But before that day could come and before any of those good things could happen, he died. He was gone. Everything could have been alright. They would have worked things out. But there was never the chance. Never the time.

At Carrbridge they can see through the mists lifting and the sun rising, the mountains white with snow.

Robbie says, "Do burglars and robbers have Christmas trees?"

"They do." Lorraine stands up. "I'm going to see if I can get a cup of coffee. Do you boys want anything?"

"What can we have?" asks John.

"How do you know?" asks Robbie. "Have you ever been in a burglar's house?"

"Not as far as I know," says Lorraine. "More often they have been in mine."

"Can we come and see and choose?" says John.

"Certainly you can. Come on, let's go." Lorraine needs to move, to do things. When they get to Edinburgh they will take a taxi. Up Dalry Road, through the traffic to the flat. Up the stairs, on with the fires, the kettle. Go for milk. Make coffee. Food. The boys can eat, unpack their Christmas toys and she, drinking the coffee, can stop. Take time. Later, she can make the phone calls.

"Then how do you know?"

"I know, Robbie," she says. "It's just something I know. Leave your bear and things on the seat, they'll be alright there till we get back. But it is something I really do know Robbie. Take my word for it. They have Christmas trees, same as we do. They have the same things."

Lorraine In Skye

Once, when I was a child, we were on holiday at my mother's mother's house on Skye and we went fishing. Evening came and the rain moved in to Waternish Bay. Then the porpoises gathered around our boat. They heaved black and huge from the sea about us.

But my father said, "Don't be afraid, they are guiding us."

And he put his arm around me and with the other he turned the outboard, turned the boat, and we came home, forever, safe to the shore.

The Laird's Beautiful Daughter

The Laird had a beautiful daughter and, in the Spring of 1892 when she was seventeen, she fell in love with a handsome horseman called Michael MacDonald. They ran away together to Glasgow. The following year, with a baby daughter, they sailed to Canada.

From Canada they travelled south for seven years until, in Shrevesport, Louisiana, they met a rich man called Martin Johnstone. They worked for him for three years, caring for his house and his carriages and his horses until, one morning in June 1904, as Michael MacDonald stood in the street below the Shrevesport & Louisiana State Bank holding the two horses while Martin Johnstone was inside, three men ran from the bank and down the steps and were fired upon from within the bank they had just robbed. One of the shots struck Michael MacDonald in the head and he was killed.

The Laird's beautiful daughter buried Michael MacDonald in Shrevesport. Two years later, when Martin Johnstone, always a restless man, moved to Dayton in Texas, she and her daughter went with him. Martin Johnstone died in 1925, no longer rich but all that he had left he gave to the Laird's daughter. She died in 1957. And after she had left Shrevesport she never went back to visit Michael MacDonald's grave because everything that remained of their life together she carried with her in her heart and she knew that wherever Michael was now, he was not in that cold and desolate, abandoned piece of ground.

In July 1988 Joan MacDonald Valente, great grand-daughter of the Laird's daughter, drove twelve miles across Houston to the house she shared with David Valente, her husband. They were going to go on holiday together for the first time in three years. They were going to talk, spend time together, see what was left of their marriage. But in the house Joan found a letter from David saying that he was in love with someone else; that he had taken everything that he wanted from the house; that whatever was left was hers, including the house. That he was sorry.

Joan did not go on holiday. She worked in Houston for another four months then she took a contract with MX-Oil who sent her first to London for two months and then, in August, to Aberdeen.

Joan loved Aberdeen. Leaving the house in the morning to the cold winds along the streets, the North Sea from her office window, grey upon grey, and a people in whom, she could sense, endurance and grim determination had been more important than optimism or hope. Mostly she worked and worked. But sometimes she would drive North out from Aberdeen, up the coast, past farms and harbours and graveyards at the edge of the sea.

Then one weekend in October she drove east, ninety miles, and at the village of Auldearn in Nairnshire she turned off the main road and drove three miles to the place called Lethen. There on a narrow road where the earth itself had risen and almost buried the old stone dykes she stepped outside the car into only the sound of the wind blowing in the trees and across the high land: A distant machine, which stopped: Then her hands on the old stones, tears cold on her face and the sky, huge, closing the road at either end, closing her life.

Joan drove from Lethen: Auldearn, Forres, Alves, Elgin, Lhanbryde, Mosstodloch, Fochabers, Keith, then, in Huntly, she stopped. In the hotel she asked for coffee, food and the yellow pages. Under genealogists she found 'MacDonald and MacDonald'.

She phoned.

"Okay," he said. "Send me a letter with anything you know

or remember. I'll get back to you in about seven days."

He sounded very cheerful, very loud on the phone. She hoped he was sober.

He phoned within the seven days.

"Your great grandmother was not related to the Laird of Lethen, not in any legitimate or recorded sense anyway, not in any records that I know of. So I'm going to concentrate on Michael MacDonald. I'll get back to you soon."

In Aberdeen the nights were darker and darker. Joan sat in her house knowing no-one outside the people at her work, not watching the TV, the inside of her head like a book she had only now opened.

John MacDonald phoned again.

"Well," he said. "A story for you. Michael MacDonald was born in Lethen in 1872. His father was a farm worker. Michael had three sisters. Two died in Scotland. Michael and the youngest sister, Helen, did not. Helen is your great grandmother's name. Her child, your grandmother Anne, was born in Glasgow in January 1893. Anne's father's name is not recorded on the birth certificate."

"Do you mean that my great grandmother and great grandfather were brother and sister?"

"No. Not necessarily. What this means is that you know now who your great grandmother was. And she was not who you thought she might be. But you do not know who the father of her child was. It might have been Michael, I suppose, but more likely not. We cannot know, or know why you have the version of the story that you have."

For a second Joan could see the narrow road in Lethen, the stones.

"Right. Thank you. Thank you for your work."

"No bother. And if you want me to take anything any further, the boat they sailed on, where they arrived in Canada? It is possible. But you know most of the story from here on. Still, if there is anything more get in touch."

Later, when even the afternoons in Aberdeen were dark, Joan phoned John MacDonald.

She said, "It is still possible she was not lying. That she was who she said she was. Maybe her mother told her."

John laughed, "Oh, you're right. Easily. That's the thing about history. No-one ever writes down the bit you really want to know. So you could be right. But I was going to phone you. I'm winding up here. You're my last client. My father needs me up North, in Nairn, back in the tractor selling business. He's getting too old to go on himself and I always said I'd go back. But before I go I was wanting to ask you out. For a meal."

"As a client?" said Joan. "I mean, to do with the work you are doing for me?"

"No. No. Not really."

"But I don't know you. I've never met you. And you don't know me."

"Och." said John. "Everyone knows me. John MacDonald. I'm forty-eight years old, long, long divorced. A wee bit fat lately right enough, and a bit ugly, but not too bad. And I know lots of your ancestors so you will not need to worry."

Two weeks later he phoned again.

"Listen. I'm leaving Aberdeen tomorrow. I'll be up North in Nairn for December. So if you still don't fancy a meal together now, how about nearer Christmas? In Nairn? Have a think about it. Can I phone you anyway? Maybe in a week?"

"All right," said Joan. "Maybe in a week."

In the second week of December Joan drives to Auldearn and, in the late afternoon darkness, parks and walks up through Lethen, round, and back to the top of the Brightmoney Brae. From here the sky is deep blue-black, bright star upon star, forever, bright dust upon dust. Out there Michael MacDonald, the handsome horseman, is dying, his life pouring out into the mud below the Shrevesport and Louisiana State Bank, the horses dancing about him. Out there Helen MacDonald, great grandmother, Michael MacDonald's sister, the Laird's beautiful daughter, arranges and rearranges the plates from all the states of America on the flowery walls of her last room where Joan, a child, is helping her, loving her. Down below, across the darkness, Joan can see a car leave a farm. Its lights dip and bounce along the track to the Auldearn Road. And she can see herself enter the Dalmore Hotel in Nairn, out of the cold, into the hall, into the warm dining room. She can see John MacDonald sitting waiting. He looks up, he sees her, gets to his feet, a large awkward man, knocking the table, spilling the water, his chair falling backwards and a waiter, carrying a tray heaped high with food, hurdling the chair gracefully as it lands in his path. He spills not a morsel, not a drop, and is applauded by the other diners, but these events are behind John MacDonald and he sees them not at all. He holds out his hands to Joan and she, taking them, laughs. They are rough, dry and warm. She cannot not laugh. She has always known that she would know him, straightaway.

While I Was Waiting For You

Two people, Jane MacKintosh and William Ross, are born in the same year, 1809, in Lethen, and grow up together as neighbours and, through their mothers, as cousins. William Ross's mother dies when he is two years old so he is as often in Jane's house as he is ever in his own. Then, in 1821, when he and Jane are twelve years old, William, a restless, reckless boy, follows his father's brother (who would never return) to sea in the Navy. Two years after this Jane's mother, who has been frail (but determined) for a long time, dies and Jane's father follows her ten months later. Jane, desolate, marries her father's partner in their haulage business, Andrew Murray, a kind, quiet, dreamy man twice Jane's age. In 1826 Jane and Andrew Murray have a baby, Margaret. Meg. And although Jane had missed William Ross when he had first gone away she had thought this ache would fade. But it does not. They are not to see each other again for fifteen years.

One morning in early February 1827, Jane is in the house with her baby, Meg, when Andrew Murray comes home. Andrew tells Jane that his stomach has been wracked since he left the house, three hours ago, by savage cramps. He is very pale and unsteady. He says he must lie down. Jane helps him to his bed. He has had these pains before, though perhaps not so bad, and he is usually well again in a day. She leaves him to sleep. Later, in the afternoon already dark, Jane's Uncle, Samuel Ross, William's father, comes to the house. He is a man with great concern for Jane, considering her as a daughter, although he is cautious of her opinions, her inclination to argue and disregard all advice. He is very anxious to see Andrew Murray, but he is reluctant to talk to Jane first. Jane goes through to Andrew but he turns away towards the wall and says he does not want to see Samuel Ross or anyone else. Jane goes back to where Samuel Ross is waiting. He is very agitated. Jane tells him he must tell her what is the matter. Samuel Ross tells her that the word is out in Lethen that Andrew Murray is in deep debt, that he owes everything that he had been thought to own. Jane asks Samuel to try to find out what he can, to find out the names of the creditors.

Jane goes back to Andrew. By now he is shivering under the blankets, his face and hair wet with sweat. He does not want to speak. A neighbour, a farmer called MacDonald, rides to Nairn for a doctor. But Andrew Murray is failing too fast. He no longer seems to recognise Jane. After two hours he cries out and a great quantity of black blood flows from his bowels and by the time the doctor comes Andrew Murray is dead.

Samuel Ross returns. He and Jane sit with Andrew Murray's body till morning when Jane sends Samuel out to begin arrangements for Andrew's funeral. She also asks Samuel about the business, what he has found out. He says that the two main creditors are James Frazer and James Logan: That he will see them as soon as he can.

In the evening Samuel returns. The house has been full of visitors all day. Whenever they can find time to be alone Jane asks Samuel what more he knows. Samuel says that James Frazer and James Logan are very shocked at the death of Andrew Murray. They had said to Samuel to tell Jane not to worry about anything till well after the funeral; that they would not wish to discuss finances in these very lamentable circumstances. But Samuel had pressed them. Knowing Jane and being reluctant to return to her without all the information, (he knew she would just send him out again) he had insisted on hearing the true situation. Samuel tells Jane that the whole haulage business, the horses and carts, all the sheds and storehouses and other property, including the house that Jane lives in, belong to James Frazer and James Logan against the money that they had lent Andrew Murray. They have sent condolences with Samuel to Jane on the death of Andrew Murray and their assurances that they will give Jane whatever time she needs to work out what to do.

Samuel Ross says Jane and Meg must come and live with him. He has plenty room with all his family gone and no knowing when William will return or whether he will return at all.

But Jane says no. She says that as soon as things can be settled here she will go to her older sister Anne in Dunvegan, Skye. Anne is married to a minister called John MacLean. She has been ill for a long time with a weakness like their mother had. Three months ago John MacLean had written to say that Anne can do less and less. Anne's own letters have only spoken of how she is expecting her second child. Jane has only met John MacLean three times. He is a handsome but closed and humourless man. This had been offset by Anne's sparkle and enthusiasm. Jane knows that these are now fading.

Four weeks after Andrew Murray's funeral Jane hands everything over to James Frazer and James Logan. Samuel Ross has retained for her a grey mare. He tells Jane he knows this horse: She is a good traveller, well used to crossing mountains and water, calm on the ferries. He says a sure-footed horse like this with a basket on either side will take Jane to Dunvegan easily. He also tells Jane that he has recruited a young drover, Duncan MacArthur, the son of an old friend, Duncan MacArthur of Stein, to guide her as far as Kyle. The young Duncan is meanwhile in Inverness and will meet them on the road. Samuel Ross has money for her, but she says she will only borrow what she needs to get her to Dunvegan and that one day she will repay him for everything.

The morning Jane Murray and Samuel Ross leave Lethen is dark and cold. Meg is wrapped, almost buried, deep in one of the baskets with those belongings that Jane has kept. They pass Nairn and walk west for seven miles where they meet the young Duncan MacArthur who has come halfway from Inverness. Duncan MacArthur is a stocky, dark, tangled haired, wild-eyed boy. He very formally greets Samuel and Jane. He is raggedy looking and carries next to nothing. Samuel Ross asks Duncan to convey greetings to his father. Samuel then holds Jane's hand for a long time. He still sees her as the slight, intense, brown-eyed child who would carry to him broken things, hurt creatures, demanding of him that they be mended. He cannot speak. But Jane laughs and tells him not to worry, they will see each other again before too long. Samuel touches the top of Meg's head then says they'd better all be going. He watches them walk away.

Duncan sets a fair pace for Inverness but Jane is glad to be moving. He tells Jane that his father has taken cattle south from Skye, through Kylerhea. Duncan will catch up with the herd after he has delivered Jane to Kyle.

Jane asks, "So where have you just been?"

Duncan says, "In the Inverness jail for the last three months."

"Why?" says Jane, "What did you do?"

"Well," he laughs. "Not much. There was a misunderstanding with some soldiers. By the nature of these things I was judged to be in the wrong."

Duncan tells Jane that as soon as he can he is going to go to America; that he has heard good reports from other highlanders.

"Will you not be sad to leave your home?" asks Jane.

"Yes," he says. "I am sure I will be sad. In fact I am sad already at the thought of it. But then it could be that sadness can carry you as far as, and even a lot further than, anything else."

"Yes," she says. "It is true. So we might be great travellers yet."

By the afternoon they are well past Inverness. The sky clears and it is bright if not warm. Duncan says he is glad to be in the open. He has been too long indoors in Inverness lately. That night they sleep for shelter at the edge of a dense wood.

The next day they are up, themselves and Meg fed, and away, shivering in the icy morning. In the afternoon they reach the river Beauly. They walk up the bank to the home of an old drover called MacRae. That night they eat hot stew with the old man who had been on the roads with Duncan's grandfather. Old MacRae's walking days are long over but he is well supplied with food and fuel by his daughters and sons. The house is warm and dry. Old MacRae shares Duncan's whisky with enthusiasm late into the night.

The morning is again clear but old MacRae warns them that the weather will turn. He says there is still snow in Glen Affric, right down to the river itself in some places.

"Make sure you are not caught in the open too late in the afternoon", he tells them.

He is proved right. By the afternoon icy rain is driving into them, the sky dark and the wind rising all the time. They are still progressing but Duncan says they should head for a shelter on the north side of the glen before the cold and wet can reach the baby Meg, buried deep and asleep in the basket. They walk steadily, soaked, to the ruin of a house with only part of the end wall still standing. A shelter is built against this wall, the earth inside dry and deep with dead bracken and grass. They secure the horse and, trying to keep warm, they settle in the rising row of the storm. Duncan says travellers do not often stop here because of the sadness of this place though he himself does not mind it.

He says, "A long time ago, when this was more of a house but even then already deserted, two children, a brother and a sister, came from the west looking for their father who was said to have been taken to Inverness after the forty five. He had been gone for many months. But these children came too late in the year and were lost or perhaps one of them injured. For whatever reason they stopped here too long, until into the winter. They never moved on. They died. When they were found they were buried together outside. In those times their father would have probably been already dead, although I don't know any more of the story."

And outside, as Duncan speaks, the storm is still rising above his voice but now they are warm enough, and the light has gone altogether so they say goodnight. Jane sleeps at first, but then she wakes with the howling wind and the terrible sadness of the dead children. In the darkness she knows that Duncan is also awake, so she gathers the sleeping Meg and crosses the floor to where he lies.

Early next day they wake, the storm is over and the sun is rising strong, the glen bright with the wet colours. Jane looks at Duncan and he looks at her, though cautiously, and she says, well, and then they both laugh. Soon they are packed and away to the west at a great speed. Jane feels more like dancing than walking and he too, the pace he is setting. Only the steadiness of the mare holds them to reason. But even she seems to move lighter on the track. And any conversations that Jane and Duncan have are short and practical as always, only with smiling and a shyness all day till evening when they stop for shelter beneath the high rocks and bed again for the night, the baby Meg warm and fed beside them.

The next day is dry again and on the third evening after this they reach Kyle. Jane is glad now to lodge at the house of the ferryman for the hot food and comfort but not when Duncan goes to stay with relatives. But he is there again early next day helping the ferryman and his two sons load the mare on to the boat and tie her down. While they all work Jane and Duncan look at each other, then do not look at each other. They are in some growing, but hidden, confusion and torment.

"It is another fine morning," says Jane to the ferryman.

"It is fine," says the ferryman, "And it will remain fine long enough for us to get you over."

Duncan walks a short distance up the beach with Jane. She thanks him for the journey they have shared.

"That we have shared more," she says, "I hope will be between ourselves only."

"It will be," answers Duncan MacArthur. "I have enough trouble with ministers and authorities and the like already, so that even were I not so fond of you as I am, and did not wish you so much goodness in life, I would be silent for my own sake."

"And God?" says Jane. "What do you think God thinks of us?"

"Oh, Jane," he says, "I am sure we have much more to fear from the same ministers and the rest of them than we will ever have to fear from God."

They shake hands as if formally, though their touch is not so, then Jane walks back down the beach. She steps on the ferry with her baby Meg. Away along the beach they can see two dogs running towards them over the stones. The dogs reach the boat and jump in. Jane asks the ferryman whose dogs they are.

He says, "They are MacDonald of Borrodale's dogs. They are on their way home."

"So where is MacDonald?" Jane asks.

"I believe he is in the south still," says the ferryman. "But wait a minute and I'll ask the dogs."

Jane laughs, but Duncan is in the water with the ferryman's sons pushing the boat out. Jane is afraid of her own laughter in case it undams the sadness inside her. If it was not for her sister Anne she would follow Duncan south.

But the ferryman says to the two dogs, "Where is MacDonald then?"

So he and the dogs look at each other for a while, the boat drifting into deeper water.

"Yes," he says taking the oars while his sons climb aboard, "They say MacDonald is still in the south. But no doubt he will follow them home soon enough."

Then he laughs and dips his oars, as his sons do, and all the while they are moving from the shore.

"Well," he says, "That's us away now. There is no one else coming that I can see."

And all the time Duncan MacArthur is left there on the more and more distant shore.

"So how will the dogs pay their fares?" asks Jane.

"Ah. Well now," says the ferryman, "It looks to me like they have forgotten to carry any money. So I expect MacDonald will have to settle their debt when he eventually passes this way."

And soon on this calm sea with steady rowing they have reached the other side. Jane steps ashore after the two dogs who run up the beach and out of sight. A silent man walks down and helps unload the horse. Jane ties the baskets on either side and settles Meg. And all the time she can see the dark, still figure of Duncan MacArthur on the other side, and sees him again each time she turns back as she leads the horse up to the road until the last time she turns and then she cannot see him anymore.

And within three years, Duncan MacArthur is in America with his brother Findlay. They travel North West to the Canadian border where they work with a family from France.

In 1834, after his brother has left to go further North into Canada, Duncan MacArthur marries Marie, the daughter of the family. They have ten children and, counting themselves and their children and the children of these children and their great grandchildren, by the time Duncan dies there are two hundred of his descendants spreading across America and Canada and beyond.

(And perhaps when Duncan MacArthur dies, and he dies a very old man in bed, his last thought is of the time he spent in the storm in Glen Affric with Jane, sheltering in the house of the dead children. But probably not. Usually when we die in bed with a good number of years behind us and a fair quantity of people around us who care that we are dying, there is no place for quiet and reflection. For it is very difficult for healthy people to rest while there is a death, while we are dying, so they are mostly busy talking or asking questions or making suggestions or disagreeing with the suggestions made by others, or putting blankets on whoever is dying, or taking them off, or adjusting other parts of the bedding or clothing or curtains, or trying to give water or other sustenance. And if there are nurses or doctors present, or both, then it is all even more active because if relatives are restless, then doctors and nurses are a thousand times worse. So while we are dying it is difficult for us to concentrate on the experience, there are so many interruptions, and it could be that we die as we have mostly lived, distracted. In fact, it could be said that, in these circumstances, we often miss our own deaths).

By the early afternoon Jane is near Broadford. The long line of a funeral approaches her. She draws the mare to the side of the road. The people at the front with the coffin are crying, some staggering with grief and having to be supported by others. But, as the procession passes Jane, at the far end of this line of mourners are young men and women, laughing, talking, jostling and pushing each other, making faces. They greet Jane as they go beyond her, gazing at her with great curiosity. She walks on for the rest of the afternoon and that evening buys board at a croft.

The crofter and his wife have nine children and a stable for the horse. They feed her and the next day their oldest boy, silent with fear of her it seems, guides Jane along the road for the first ten miles. He then points out her way between the sea and the hills, turns and walks back the way they had come. Later, a huge man on a horse directs her to a widow's house for the night. The widow is a broken looking, sad woman but she is very kind to Jane and Meg. She feeds them soup and bread, thinning the soup for Meg. The next day she tells Jane where to go, but as there is only one path, Jane feels there is not much chance of being lost. In the late afternoon she sees two eagles very high in the sky and she watches them till she can see them no more. Then distance, sadness and loneliness empty her, weaken her. She takes Meg from the basket and sits on a stone, holding and hugging the baby for a long time until she can stand up again and keep walking. That night, at another lodging, she sleeps a long deep sleep and wakes in the morning, the grief still in her body, but better able to keep going. This is the day she reaches her sister's house in Dunvegan.

Jane ties the horse and takes Meg from the basket. The door of the manse opens and her brother-in-law, the minister John MacLean, is standing there. Although he is a tall man he is thin and frail. He is not many years past thirty but his face is marred by shadows. He comes forward to help Jane.

He says, "Go straight to see your sister. She will be very glad to see you."

Chrissie, the servant girl, an orphan, almost a child still, comes from the back of the house. She is very shy, nervous. She nods but she does not speak. She takes the horse round to the stable.

Jane goes to the room where her sister Anne is lying, her new baby by her side. Rachel, her first child, is playing on the floor. Jane holds Anne, who seems like only bones inside the blankets.

"Oh Anne," she says and never wants to let her go. Anne's face and hands are very cold. In the emotion Rachel comes and sits close to her mother.

Anne says, "It is very foolish. I cannot grasp or hold anything anymore. I am dropping everything. Perhaps my hands might get better again but I don't know. Walking is sometimes very difficult and sometimes it is alright. But even when I can walk, I can't climb stairs at all. Isn't it daft? That is why I am down here. Look, see, this is our new baby, Leah. Isn't she beautiful? But I am not feeding her very well."

"No, she looks fine," says Jane. "And here is Meg. I have enough to feed Leah and Meg both if need be. But we need to warm you up as well. We'll get a fire going in here."

Although the married couple, the MacDonalds, who work for the manse, and Chrissie, the young girl, have tried hard and done their best there is a feeling of hopelessness and neglect in the house. The illness of Anne and the unhappiness of John MacLean is like a paralysis over everything. With Chrissie to help, Jane looks after her sister and the children during the day and evening while the MacDonalds attend to the house. At these times John MacLean does his parish work, then each night he spends with Anne, talking, sleeping sometimes, caring for her. With Jane in the house, Anne is much more peaceful, and everything is better organised, the children playing and happy.

Spring arrives and the weather is warmer.

Three months later Jane tells her sister, then her brother-in-law, that she is going to have another baby. John MacLean says that she must be very glad that she will have her dead husband's child. Perhaps, he says, it will be a son who can carry Andrew Murray's name. Jane agrees that she is glad. She keeps to herself the knowledge that this is not Andrew Murray's child.

Jane stays strong and well throughout her pregnancy and Anne seems to get no worse. She can even walk again with some assistance. Chrissie and Jane help her outside where she watches the summer pass and a mild autumn arrive. But with winter she again deteriorates.

Early in the New Year Jane's baby is born. A girl. Jane calls her Anne. Now there are four children in the house. Anne is a fat, happy, easy baby. But Jane' sister Anne is failing all the time. John MacLean hardly leaves her bedside anymore.

At the end of May, late in the night, John MacLean wakes Jane. They wake no-one else but Chrissie hears, or senses, the crisis and follows them to Anne's room. Jane and Chrissie sit on one side, and John MacLean on the other, of Anne as she dies.

Until and after the funeral, the dark crowds and elders all around, and then the emptiness, John MacLean hardly eats or speaks at all. He is either in his room or out walking. He does not seem to sleep anymore. He is gaunt and crazed looking, gray and ruined like a death himself.

Then one night, two months after her sister's death, Jane is woken by a sound outside her room. In the darkness she crosses in the cold and opens the door. Outside is John MacLean. She hears his breathing, hard and staggered. He tries, his voice like a broken cry, but he cannot speak. Jane whispers, what is wrong? Is anything wrong? She can hardly see him but she can feel him shuddering. She is flooded by frailty and grief for them all, for her sister, the children and John MacLean. And for herself. She is crying and reaches out her hands from all this desolation and she takes him in.

The next day John MacLean is at work again in his parish, wild with energy to sort out the neglect of months. He is organising meetings, visits, ensconced in church business and arrangements with elders.

In two weeks he comes again to Jane's door. And again and again. They never speak of these times. During the days of work they maintain their formal relationship and at night lie together in each other's warmth, but without the language to speak of what is happening.

Jane keeps going, keeps working, for months, into the Autumn, not knowing what else to do. She knows that the situation cannot continue. She does not want it to continue. She is haunted by unease and deceit. Then she realises that she is again pregnant. Now it is clear that before long they will all be plunged into disaster and public disgrace. She tells John MacLean. He is very calm about their predicament.

The next day he tells Jane that there is a house in Glasgow left to him and his brother Thomas by an uncle. Thomas is in America. Before Jane's condition can become visible, Jane and Chrissie must take the children and go there. John MacLean will follow as soon as he can.

In the fifth month of her pregnancy Jane, Chrissie and the four children sail to Glasgow. They stay in lodgings while they open and prepare the house. Chrissie, with no English, and having never been more than fifteen miles beyond Dunvegan before, takes to the change with extraordinary enthusiasm and sometimes terror. But through Chrissie's excitement Jane is also released into the adventure and their energy carries the children. After three months John MacLean joins them. It is understood in Dunvegan that he is broken by the death of his wife and in fact this, with the loss of his occupation, becomes more and more true in Glasgow.

In June 1829, Jane has another daughter. Jane calls this child Catherine after her own mother.

But John MacLean is now a tortured and difficult man. He tells Jane disgrace is not far behind them in Glasgow, so full of highlanders, and that they must go far away and start again in America. But Jane says this will not happen: That there can be no new start for her and John MacLean. The division between them is already wide and can only grow more. She says his guilt and misery about his religion and about his dead wife, Jane's sister Anne, and his continuing love of Anne, will always be stronger than anything they could ever make together: That if he wants to go to America, and she understands that in the circumstances he probably must, then he should go without her. And if he goes without her then he must go without his children. She says if he goes and eventually settles then they will see what is best for his daughters.

"I will stay here and Chrissie and I will reorganise this house to take in lodgers. With this and with whatever money you chose, or are able, to leave us, we will manage".

John MacLean argues and continues, torn and oppressed, for another five months but, separated from his religion and his colleagues by his situation and by the rumours that are growing amongst those with whom he would normally mix, in October 1829 he leaves for America. The last time Jane sees John MacLean in this life he is on a ship full of emigrants sailing from the Clyde. And she is not even sure whether the figure she is waving to amongst the crowds on the decks of the ship, and pointing out to the children, is John MacLean or not. Chrissie tells Jane afterwards that she thinks Jane was pointing at the wrong man.

John MacLean lands in Wilmington, North Carolina. He spends his first year working as a clerk for a shipping company. However he becomes increasingly involved with the church. Eventually he travels upriver to a settlement called Broken Creek where he begins to preach again. In time his powerful and intense sermons, his passion and energy in the pulpit, contrasted with his humility, kindness and serious gentleness when visiting his parishioners, gain him a regular congregation. He is a popular and unusually loved minister. He carries with him an atmosphere of separateness and sadness that attract many to him and he returns their devotion with all the vigour that he has. There are few days when he does not work himself to the point of collapse. All around he is seen as a very special and very good man.

In the Autumn of 1834 John comes out alone, late in the evening, from a meeting with his elders and sees, already high over the trees, the moon, vast and yellow, and he is stopped, invaded, by a flood of pure happiness in his blood and in his mind for the first time in his life: An extraordinary warmth that is gone as soon as it is there.

But something stays with him: The possibility of something different in this world and he thinks, for the first time without guilt, of his three daughters and of Jane. Late that night in his room he writes to Jane to say he has a place for them all, all the children, herself, Chrissie, if they will come.

From Glasgow Jane eventually writes back in answer to his request. She knows Rachel and Leah should go. They are his daughters and not hers. But her heart would break and perhaps theirs too. So she would have to go with them. But she does not want to.

The exchange of letters between Jane Murray and John MacLean is slow and seven months later they have just begun negotiating, he with optimism, she without joy, but trying to find a way to be fair, to be just, when a farmer, Simon Gilchrist, rides to the church where John MacLean has just preached and is standing at the door of the meeting place talking with his congregation as they leave. Simon Gilchrist's wife, Caroline, has been, for two years, ill with grief at the loss of their ten year old only son, only child, killed by a horse. She goes often to see John MacLean to talk and to cry. Caroline Gilchrist hardly speaks any more to her husband nor he to her.

Simon Gilchrist rides up through the crowd. He dismounts and walks straight up to John MacLean. He stabs John MacLean through the heart and turns away, leaving John dying on the ground. Simon Gilchrist rides off to the west (it is believed). He is never seen again. John MacLean is carried back inside but he is dead without speaking or opening his eyes. Caroline Gilchrist, who had been beside John MacLean when he was killed by her husband, walks home to her empty house, her left sleeve and down her dress, her forehead and left ear and even her shoes soaked with John MacLean's blood.

She sits in the quietness of her kitchen, not lighting any lamps, watching the darkness arrive like a friend. Armed men come to the house but they see Simon Gilchrist is not there. They ask her if she needs anything. She says no. They leave one man to wait all night and into the next day but Simon Gilchrist never returns.

Eight years later Caroline marries a grain merchant and horse dealer, an owner of land, called George Glass. They have three sons, George, Frank and Henry. George and Frank are killed in 1862 in the civil war, at Shiloh. Henry dies in a New York theatre in 1931 during a musical evening. He often sleeps during these performances so his wife and daughter do not realise he is dead until the end when they rise to leave. He is 85 years old.

When Jane hears of the death of John MacLean she tells Chrissie she would like to move North again. Her sense of division and uncertainty is now gone. There are only the seven of them now: Jane, Chrissie, and the five girls. Perhaps eight. Robert Farquharson, a boy who had been hired occasionally to do odd jobs at the lodging house, then seemed to be around most of the time, besotted with Chrissie since the first moment he saw her, also immediately plans to move North with them whenever, or wherever, they decide to go.

Jane sells her very successful business in Glasgow (John's brother Thomas who should have had a half share in this sale has not been heard of for twelve years and, with his wild ways, has been long assumed dead, either hung or otherwise killed).

In the spring of 1835 they move North to Inverness. They buy another house beside the river, and new clothes for Robert Farquharson whose rags Chrissie has just begun to notice along with the deep green of his eyes.

In June 1835 Jane is walking home. The children are behind with Robert, either pulling or pushing the cart of provisions for the lodging house, their new venture. Wee Catherine is dawdling with Chrissie a while behind all this. Jane, since her return North, has visited Samuel Ross twice and been visited by him four times. He is elated by her return and often nearly overwhelmed by emotion when he sees her. He tells her that William was injured in a skirmish at sea and has been in a hospital for many months, but that he is recovering and will return North as soon as he is able enough to travel.

Jane looks back to see if the children are keeping up. She turns again and walking towards her down the riverbank she sees William Ross. They approach each other steadily though William is moving awkwardly using a walking stick. They are soon close (it also seems to take a long time) and stop face to face.

"A fine day, Mrs Murray," William says, "And that is a fine puckle of bairns you have there. Are they all your own?"

"As good as," says Jane. "But once you called me Jane. Am I now to call you Mr Ross?"

"I don't know," he says. "The last time we saw each other we were still bairns ourselves. A lot has gone by since then."

"Well," she says, "We were bairns right enough. But we were also the best of friends. Now that we are grown can that friendship not be kept?"

"Oh it can be, it can be," he says. "And it would be very dear to me if it could be."

"Then we are," she says. "You are William again and I am Jane."

"We are," he says. "Thank God, Jane, we are."

And the control that she had maintained so far over the muscles of her face is almost lost when he says her name as if she had held that control not for just minutes but for most of her life. To keep what is left of a grip on herself, Jane says sternly, "You are missing an eye, William. Unless it is still there underneath that black patch?"

"No," he says. "You are right. It is gone. And with it a portion of my leg. I thought I should quit the sea before I lost anything else."

"I think you are very wise, William," she says. "To remain so nearly intact. And how are things in Lethen? Do they talk of me at all? Do they consider how I came by all these bairns?"

(She asks him what they think of her in Lethen but at the same time she knows, as he knows she knows, that in Lethen facts or details or realities relating to any situation are merely the base material supplied by God. It is the clay. The pot is still to be made. It is considered in Lethen up to us to arrange these formless lumps, disorganised bits, to alter them, add to them or subtract from them as need be, smooth and edge them if necessary, to give them a shape that is clear and makes a sense that will hold the listener who might, himself or herself, also see some further adjustments or improvements that are required to refine that rough version that they have received, that they now consider is lacking or inadequate here or there).

"Well, Jane," says William carefully, "It seems generally agreed from everything that I hear said in Lethen, that you came by all these bairns by kindness."

(William does not say that in those cases where there had been less favourable talk about Jane, his father first, and then William himself on his return, have offered to shoot or by some other means kill, or at least permanently maim, the miserable, cynical and worthless speaker. And it is suddenly then remembered by such speakers that the ancestors of Samuel and William had, not many generations back, maybe two or three, a reputation, whether deserved or not, for unpredictable and excessive violence.)

"And what do you say William?" asks Jane (for this is what she really needs to know) "That I have brought back so many?"

"Jane," he says, "Whatever you bring I would see more of, if it means I see more of you."

By now they are breathing too fast so that their voices are breaking strangely and to themselves sound not even like their own. And within each of their chests is a heart like something boiling in a tightly lidded pan.

"William. You can see as much of me as you ever want to," she says.

And William is leaning, as if casually, against a wall; but in fact even his good leg is weak with hope and he is anxious not to show his lack of balance.

"Is today and tomorrow and the next day too soon, Jane?" he asks.

Jane is laughing now (a safer release, she has decided, than crying, even with happiness, which she knows now she can do also at almost any later date) and trying not to twirl about.

"Yesterday or last week or last year would not have been too soon, William," she says. "If you had never gone away at all, would not have been too soon. But look, now we are deserted. (Chrissie and Robert have forced the curious children on ahead) We will have to catch up with all these bairns that you say you would like to see more of. See, wee Catherine is waiting. She will not allow Chrissie to progress any further without us. So we will go to the house and find you something to eat and drink and we will catch up with the news of all your adventures and injuries."

So they hurry after the rest of the family.

"Jane," says William later, sitting in Jane's crowded kitchen. "What were we doing with all those years? What happened that we missed so much time?"

"Well," says Jane, busy with huge utensils on the roaring stove. "While I was waiting for you to come back, I went for a walk."

So, not many months later, they marry (as eventually do Chrissie and Robert) and go to live in Lethen (Chrissie and Robert stay on in the house in Inverness) where with all the good food and fine air they proceed to have seven more children, bringing the numbers up to twelve (Chrissie and Robert have eight) which is considered in Lethen to be a reasonable number to account for and balance the vicissitudes of disease, accident and deliberate harm that tend to reduce our human numbers, making our years often unreasonably short.

And although William is not Jane's last husband (she is a warm and companionable woman and men seem mostly, if not always, to die soonest) he is always the main one. He is the one that she hopes will be waiting for her when she dies and who she will lie with again, but in Heaven.

Hobart

The afternoon of the day I met Hobart the Pottery toilet had been blocked since the morning. I had given up poking at it with the piece of bent fence wire I keep especially for this job. I phoned Dolores.

"It's been blocked all day Dolores and I can't shift it at all."

Dolores said, "I'll phone the plumbers."

A while later, maybe an hour, Mary-Anne and Lucille, who make the dinners, came into the Pottery. They were clinging together, laughing and singing.

"Oh, oh, oh, what a hunk. Who is that gorgeous man in your toilet, Dugal?"

I said, "It's the plumber."

"Cor, he is so handsome," said Mary-Anne and Lucille.

"Really?" I said. Outwardly with cold indifference. Inside I was very annoyed. I do not like to hear that other men are handsome.

Then Janet came in.

"Dugal, Dugal, do you know what is down the stairs sitting in James MacLeod's blue Ford Escort van?"

I said, "Another handsome plumber?"

"No, no", she said, "it's a bull terrier."

"No," I said. "It's not, is it? A bull terrier? In the van?"

"Yes," Janet said. "Yes it is, really it is. A bull terrier. It's a bull terrier."

I went down the stair and there, out on Horne Terrace, sat in the plumber's blue Escort van was a white and brown bull terrier. I went closer to the van. I looked in the window. He looked back at me. He narrowed his eyes. I fell in love.

The plumber came downstairs. He was certainly very handsome. He was almost as good looking as I was myself at his age. He was perhaps a bit tall. I believe the best looking men are always about five foot seven and a quarter inches tall.

He said, "That's your toilet clear again."

I said, "Thanks, great, thanks very much. Here, is this your bull terrier? What's his name? How old is he? What a great dog."

The handsome plumber said, "His name is Hobart. He's ten months old."

I said, "He's wonderful. He is really great. What a great dog."

The handsome plumber put his rods in the back of the blue Ford Escort van.

He said, "Got to go."

He drove off with Hobart up Horne Terrace.

The Pottery toilet was often blocked in the next year. Whenever it was, half the folk from the Pottery Workshop joined Mary-Anne and Lucille cheering and clapping the handsome plumber when he arrived, admiring him while he worked, and saying to him, "Aren't you wonderful."

The rest of us would be down the stair at the blue Ford Escort van. We gazed at Hobart through the glass. Hobart always looked back but I did not know what he thought or what he felt.

In July we closed for the holidays. We were three days back when the Pottery was blocked again. I phoned Dolores.

"What's the problem with your toilet, Dugal?" she said. "The plumber's bills are pretty steep for this year."

I said, "Sorry Dolores, I'll try to keep my eye on it."

When the handsome plumber arrived I went down to the van to see Hobart. I knew I could not go on meeting him like this now that Dolores was suspicious. I think he sensed something. I saw a glint in his eye that might have been a tear, although bull terriers have such tiny eyes it was hard to tell. We managed not to block the toilet for three weeks. Then I had to phone Dolores.

"The toilet is blocked again Dolores. God knows what happened this time."

Dolores said, "I'll phone James MacLeod's."

The handsome plumber came up the stair and I went down the stair to the van. Hobart was not in the passenger seat. I ran back up the stairs and pushed through the crowd watching the handsome plumber in the toilet.

"Where is Hobart?" I asked him.

"He broke his leg," said the handsome plumber. "He fell down the stairs at home. He has been in plaster for three weeks and it will be another three before it comes off, so he cannot come to work with me."

"I'm awful sorry," I said. "God, that's awful. I hope he will be alright. Give him my regards. I hope it is not too painful."

"Och. The vet says he will be fine," said the handsome plumber. "He'll recover no bother."

An hour later Dolores phoned.

She said, "The next time your toilet gets blocked one of the plumbers will come in from James MacLeod's and he will show you how to use the rods to unblock the toilet. He will leave you a set of rods so you can always unblock your own toilet from now on."

"Thanks, Dolores," I said.

A week later the handsome plumber came in and taught me how to unblock the toilet. He handed me over a set of rods and I handed him a get well card for Hobart.

He said, "Thanks."

We went down the stairs to the van.

Before he drove off he said, "You know, every time I go home from work there is a visitor in to see Hobart. My mother worries about him all the time. She carries him out to see the grass ten times a day. The phone never stops ringing. There are forty-seven get well cards on the mantelpiece already."

He drove off. As I watched the blue Ford Escort van go off up Horne Terrace I was remembering what the handsome plumber's boss once said to me.

He said, "If you go on putting clay down your sinks you are

going to plug up the whole system. It's terrible stuff, clay in pipes. It would take us weeks to put the whole thing right."

"God," I said. "No kidding? Weeks? You mean it would take weeks?"

"Aye," said the handsome plumber's boss. "That's right, it would. More than weeks."

Love And Machinery

It is the end of November. Dark nights. Harriet is putting wee Jakey to bed. He is three years old. She waits with him till he is asleep then goes back through to the room where her boyfriend, Roddy, is on the sofa, feet up, but not watching the TV.

Harriet sits down. She and Roddy have been together eight months. He has his own place but he stays with Harriet most of the time. He is looking at the ceiling, hands behind his head, not speaking.

Harriet says, "Are you ok?"

"Look." He says. "We never go out anymore. Your mother would babysit for us if we wanted, only you always say she can't because she's already babysitting Jake for you three days a week when you are at the art school. But now I'm working the different nights he could be with me the three days. Or some of the time, anyway. Then your mother could be here some nights, or say even at weekends, so we could go out."

"But maybe your times will change," says Harriet. "So that would be no good. And my mother is used to this arrangement. This routine. I mean maybe she wouldn't be happy coming out at nights. Also I have to keep going with all the stuff I've got to do for the art school. The projects and that. It's not enough just turning up the three days a week. Well, not for me anyway. Everything takes me a long time."

"Well, I think you could work something out if you really wanted to. And my times'll not change for a good while yet, so even for now. Or you could ask your mother for just one night a week as a start. It'd be better than nothing. Right now this is deadly. Every night in."

"Look," says Harriet. "It's only another few weeks till the holidays. Three. We could sort all this out then. Maybe we could work out a new routine for after the New Year."

"God. The New Year. That'll be another thing," he says. But he doesn't say anymore. He picks up the paper, switches on the TV.

Three months later, March, Harriet is drinking coffee with her friend Lucy.

Lucy asks, "Do you never see him at all anymore?"

"No," says Harriet. "Not at all. It's all well and truly over."

"But why?" asks Lucy. "Just because of the going out? And you like a night out more than anyone. I bet you've been on more night outs since he left than you ever were with him."

"More? Do you think so?" says Harriet. "No. Well. Maybe. But it wasn't just the going out that was a problem. It wasn't just that."

"So what was it then?" encourages Lucy, intrigued. "He seemed a really nice bloke as well as his looks. The nicest yet I would have said."

"Well. That's true. But anyway." Harriet is looking away.

"So come on then. What was wrong?" asks Lucy, not letting go.

"Well. Ok. This is going to sound crazy. I know it is. It's just that, well, sometimes, I mean, don't say this to anyone else, it wouldn't be fair on him. So don't ever say anything. I mean, poor Roddy, it's me, I know, not him. Anyway. But you hear about it in the papers, on the TV, all the time. I mean about men who kill children. Or other things they do. I mean children who are not theirs. But not strangers. It's if you have a child, I think, who is from someone you were with before him. That's what seems to be the problem. So I think that's what it was. I know it's really daft but I think that's what was wrong. Well, with me anyway."

"God," says Lucy. "That is definitely, definitely crazy. Surely there were never any signs of anything like that? Roddy was really nice. He was really, really nice. He was not like that at all. He was an easy-going kind of person. You never thought he would harm Jakey, did you? I mean, did you really? He was never violent or anything was he? Ever? Or to you or anything?"

"No, no," says Harriet. "No, he wasn't. He was alright that way always, Roddy. No, to be fair, it was never that he showed any signs that's what he might do. No. Never. Never. It was not like that at all. He was ok, Roddy. He was fine."

"So what was it then?"

"Well. Ok. Maybe I am crazy. Or maybe even if there had just been the two of us he wasn't the right one anyway. But it was like I was stuck all the time. Weighed down. And I knew that going back to the art school, even with Jakey, was my own choice. So it wasn't like I had to. And it wasn't as if I really thought that Roddy would harm Jakey ever. It was never that so much. It was just that, well, ok, it was just that I was never, in all that time, I was never getting any surer that he wouldn't."

The first Saturday after Easter, cold and bright outside, Harriet is in the Art School early waiting for her mother, Estelle, to collect Jakey. As soon as they have gone Harriet is going to mix a pile of clay ready for the work she means to do over the next few weeks. She is going to hand build some really big stuff. Vessels. Simple but big. Even huge.

Estelle is late. Jakey will not settle and wait. He is having too good a time running round the tables and wheels where a third year student, Al, has been throwing wide cylinders: He will join them together later into tall shapes like stacks of battered dustbins. Harriet likes Al's work; the dirty, muddy, dry, sometimes metallic, glazes. Al has stopped throwing and is talking to Jakey who is already covered with clay from the wheels.

Harriet says, "I'm sorry, Al. Is he stopping you working? My mother's supposed to be coming to collect him but she's a bit late. Jakey likes it here and usually it's ok at weekends, only not today because I've got to mix clay and he can't be around with all the clay dust. Silicosis and all that."

"No, it's alright," says Al. "He's no bother. In fact I'm enjoying his company. I'm finished making all the stuff I need for now. I'll just let them dry out a bit then I'll cover them till Monday. They'll be fine. So how old's Jakey? He looks about the same age as my brother. About three? Is he?"

"He is. He's three," says Harriet. "And a half. But isn't that a big gap in ages between you and your own wee brother?"

"Well he's really my half brother," says Al. "My mother married again. When I was twelve. And I've got two half sisters of seven and eight as well. They're great. I miss them while I'm here."

Estelle arrives. Flustered. The wrong bus.

"It's my brain I think," she says. "I must've read the numbers back to front."

She takes Jakey away shopping. Jakey is reluctant. He is having too good a time with Al's clay. But Estelle encourages him. Bribes.

Harriet makes coffee before she starts on the clay. And one for Al. They are sitting on the clay bags drinking.

"How was it, your mother marrying again?" Harriet asks. "Was that ok?"

"It was great," Al laughs. "It took a lot of the focus off me. You know what it's like. At that age. Your mother. I mean, when you're twelve. And I knew my step dad already for a long time. So he was no bother. Actually, he's great. And the house full of folk again. It suited me just fine. And my mother. I could see that. So. No. It's never been a problem. In fact just the opposite. I've been lucky. It's been fine. Just fine. But look, I'll tell you what, would you like a hand mixing your clay? I'm finished my own stuff right now. I've just to cover it up. Unless you are going to be mixing some secret formula or something? Otherwise I'll give you a hand."

"No, no, that would be really good," says Harriet. "Really a lot of help. Then you can do some of the digging of the clay out of the machine when it's finished mixing. That's the bad bit.

That's the bit I don't like. Too much of a struggle. So that's a great offer."

They finish the coffee and go across to the mixing room. Harriet puts on a dust mask. She gives one to Al. She looks in her notebook. She takes a 25kg bag of ball clay and gets Al to carry another over to the Cruickshank.

The Cruickshank is an old, very battered, rusty blue, ex-bakery, dough-mixing machine. It has been in the ceramics department for thirty years. And was probably in a bakery for thirty years before that. Inside the huge flat sided bowl are two s-shaped arms. When the Cruickshank is going these rotate at different speeds in opposite directions, weaving together but never touching.

Harriet splits open the clay bags with a knife. She and Al tip them into the mixing bowl. She adds a half bag of china clay and a bucket measure of sixty mesh grog and starts the machine, engaging the rusty gear handle at the left side of the Cruickshank. The two arms inside the bowl shudder and begin churning, the whole mechanism clattering and shaking, the soft, powdered clay dust billowing up and over Harriet and Al. They are looking into the floating, mingling, grey and white clouds. They can't speak anymore because of the masks and the rumbling racket of the Cruickshank but they are lulled and relaxed by the rhythmic, tumbling, compounding motion. They are comfortable. Dreamy. Content.

And down in the town, in a Shelter charity shop, Estelle feels dizzy, and a pain so strange that she is not even sure is part of her but instead passing her like an intense flash of light, hardly seen, or the cold wake of a fast train already gone. She sits down on a three legged table, marked two pounds fifty, near where Jakey, for the first time since he was born, falls in love, a love that is to illuminate his whole life, with a yellow toy digger, rubber tracked.

And this strangeness that Estelle feels is the beginning of a failure of her heart that will kill her twenty eight months later.

In hospital, in her last days, articulate though very weak, she tells Harriet that, in this life she is soon to be leaving, she wishes she had danced more. She says to Harriet that she believes that, in any life, you cannot dance too often or too long. And the love that Jakey feels for the battered, chipped toy is the beginning of something that grows from this moment and, twenty six years later, he has become a virtuoso, a magician, of huge road building, rock crushing, tunnel digging, mountain moving machines. He, it is said, finds it easier to make a JCB dance than he does his own feet and that he can thread a needle or write his own name more dextrously with the long arm of a 3CX than he can with his own hand. Then, one rainy day, a black-eyed young woman, Eilidh, a teacher from the far western edge of the Island of Lewis, looking through the misted window of a school in Glasgow where a new playground is being built, sees the balletic grace of the metal giant as it tears asunder the old cracked tar surfaces and she falls in love with the weathered, cheerful face of its operator and (as she is to say fourteen months on from this first sighting, glorious in magnolia and forty shades of green at their wedding) for her, truly, the earth moves.

Entranced, Harriet and Al have watched the dry clay tumbling for ten minutes. Eventually Harriet breaks away. She fills a bucket with water, brings it over and pours it into the mix.

And gradually the buoyant clay powder thickens and becomes heavy, the water sloshing the dust down into large awkward crusted clods, like those turned up by a plough, separating, then rammed squelching into each other, pushed under and swallowed by the opposite movements of the arms.

Harriet adds more water to the continuously dividing and colliding mass. Steadily the wrestling confusion of crumbling dryness and clotting lumps blends into a smooth rolling union of sloppy, gurgling, convulsive limbs of clay, the faster of the two arms relentlessly thrusting the creamy mounds round and down into the more languorous rising of the second arm.

Then the soft clouds of nearly weightless particles are gone, like smoke clearing. Al looks across the heaving machine. He can see Harriet's eyes between her mask and her ragged fringe of brown hair. He had begun to notice her often, months ago, while she worked, purposeful, on her precarious constructions, her body lost in a baggy boiler suit, or relaxed, rolling cigarettes, long earrings swinging as she licked the paper, or while she painted, daubing and sweeping slow swollen brushfuls of dark dripping red iron oxide across her scarred clay surfaces.

She is looking back at him. He feels his face grow warm, his ears reddening and hot. She is saying something but with the muffling of the dust mask and the tumult of the Cruickshank he cannot hear what it is. But he knows she is smiling behind the mask. He can imagine her mouth, her teeth, and he wonders what has made her smile. What she is thinking.

Harriet stops the machine. There is a sudden, but not dead, silence. She reaches over into the bowl, digging her fingers deep into the soft new clay. She pulls out a wad. She squeezes it between her fingers, rolls it between her palms, then throws it back in the mix.

She takes off her mask. "That's fine. That's about right. It's ok."

She looks over at Al, and reaches in again for the clay. She rolls a handful into a ball and holds it out.

"Here," she says. "What do you think? Do you think this is good enough?"

Al pulls off his mask. He reaches out to her and takes the clay.

"It seems fine to me," he says. "Harriet. Actually, very good. Really good. If it was for me I'd be very happy."

"Well, if you're happy," she laughs, his young face, although she is only four years older, "I'm happy too. I'll just give it a few more minutes, then we'll turf it out."

So the rumbling starts again, the vibrations of the old Cruickshank. And the shouts of the children in the streets below. These are the sounds she will remember in all the days and years that she and Al will be together.

But this is not the first time that she knows she will love him. Two months before, in winter, she had stayed late in the art school finishing a pot, painting into the growing dark, and, although she hardly knew him then, she had felt at peace because he was there, working, in the same room.

Drumelzier

Aileen is clever in school, in Nairn Academy. She passes all her exams and goes away to the University in Aberdeen. She does well in her first year, comes home for the summer and works in a hotel. She sees all her old friends. In the autumn she goes back to Aberdeen for her second year. Two weeks later her mother dies.

Aileen comes home for the funeral. Three weeks later she goes back to Aberdeen but she lasts only a few days. She comes home again to Nairn and this time she does not leave for fourteen years.

Aileen's father, Walter, has never done much in the house. Eventually Aileen does all the cooking, shopping, cleaning. Walter comes home, eats, goes out four nights a week to the Station Hotel, drinking with his friends. He worries about Aileen, his only child, but they do not manage to talk and soon he does not ask her any more when she will go back to Aberdeen, start up her life again. And it is not only to Walter that she does not speak. She works in the house in the mornings and sees no one if she can help it. In the afternoons and evenings, as long as there is light, and sometimes when the light has gone, she goes far along the beaches, far up the country roads, the river, the woods, in the rain, in all the seasons.

Walter drinks, perhaps not too much, but steadily. Never violent or troublesome, sometimes he comes home very late. Aileen is upstairs in bed. She can hear him downstairs singing and crying for his dead wife, his loneliness, into the night.

One day, when Aileen is thirty-three years old, one of her father's friends comes from the garage and says that Walter has been taken in the ambulance. He is unconscious, maybe a stroke.

Walter lies in Nairn Hospital. For three weeks Aileen sits by his bed every day. She goes for walks sometimes and goes home at night only half a mile away. The rest of the time she is beside her father. He never wakes. One afternoon, when Aileen is out along the river for an hour, Walter dies.

After the funeral Walter's friends come back to the house. Aileen puts out the sandwiches and pours the whisky. They sit awkwardly. They stay as long as they think will be alright, enough. They are anxious to be gone to the Station Hotel, to miss Walter in one of the places they will miss him most. They are anxious to test themselves against his empty place, to make something that includes his absence where they can drink and laugh again. They are kind men but they need to get away from Aileen, to take with them her reassurance that she will be alright, that she does not need them, that she is managing fine, that everything will be ok, that she is tired now and will have an early night, that they can go and leave her.

Aileen is glad when she is alone.

In Aberdeen, fourteen years before, Aileen had a friend, Jennifer, and after Aileen had left Aberdeen and never come back, Jennifer would come to Nairn to see her, maybe once every month for a weekend and then, later, after three years, when Jennifer was finished her course and she too had left Aberdeen, they would write: Aileen's letters a careful relating of weather and walks, things seen and books read, films on television: Jennifer's a chaotic, emotional, confused testimony of her enthusiastic and always dramatically unsuccessful relationships: A record of her, by herself unrecognised, resilience throughout bad choices and of her character whose optimism was encouraged and fed by bad luck as if there could only be so much bad luck for one person and if you were to battle through your share you would then have nothing but good luck left. And as well as the letters, Jennifer usually managed to visit at least once a year, and sometimes more, when she was with some touring theatre company going round

Caithness and the outer Isles, or, for two years, when she was with a band, although not playing any musical instruments or singing.

At the times Jennifer came to stay, Aileen would cook a special meal and Walter would bring home whisky, beer and, especially for Jennifer, dark expensive vintage port. They would eat and talk and laugh till late, Jennifer's wild curls swinging with delight, till dawn, and the next day they would go out in the car someplace, to Loch Ness or to the Black Isle. Or Carrbridge, to the mountains. They would eat scones and cakes in a hotel and walk on the moors across the heather.

After Jennifer had gone Walter would try to keep the companionship, the warmth, the good feeling, going. He would talk to Aileen about the same things the three of them had enjoyed. But Aileen would start going to her room again. She would go out alone again, walking.

After Walter's funeral, after the men have gone, Aileen phones Jennifer. She had tried phoning some three days before but there had been no answer. But this time Jennifer is there. Aileen tells Jennifer that Walter is dead. She says to Jennifer, "You know you are always saying for me to come and stay with you at your place sometime? Well, can I come now?"

Jennifer stays thirty miles south of Edinburgh, two hundred miles south of Nairn, in a cottage rented from a farmer, at a place called Drumelzier on the River Tweed, the dark hills all about, and on them razed and broken stone forts, hunting birds far in the sky, sheep and bones and wild tattooed shepherds racing battered motor bikes across old battle grounds, their tattered collie dogs riding at their backs.

Aileen arrives late, already into the night.

Jennifer says, "I've just been in London. I had the interview, did I tell you? And I got in. What a shock. I've to be down there to start in three weeks. And it's a year's course. Well, eight months. God knows what I'll do with the cottage. I don't want to lose it. And then there's Bob. But you've not met him yet."

They go round the back of the cottage in the dark and there, coming out of a barrel set on its side against the stone dyke, is an old thin dog, his eyes like glass in the torchlight, his tail waving slowly.

"He was the retired shepherd's dog, who had the house before me, who died, and when I took on the cottage they were going to get the vet to take Bob away to put him down, he was already sixteen then, but it seemed a shame when I saw him and he's no bother so I've had him since then and he's nearly twenty now. But he won't come into the house. Ever. He just comes to the door and looks in, even in the snow or winter or gales. And it gets really cold here, along the Tweed. He had a stroke about a year ago and I thought that was it. I thought that was the end of him, but he's still here. And he gets about fine though he is weak on the left side."

Bob is sniffing about, looking at Aileen (but pretending not to) now and then. He is very shy, a brown and white collie, and taller than the black and white farm collies Aileen knows up North. Aileen strokes his back, his coat sparse and rough, the bones of his spine.

"The farmer says Bob has a bit of the old bearded collie in him," says Jennifer. "But I can't go south and leave him or that'll be the end of him. No one wants an old dog and anyway this is the only place he's ever lived. He couldn't move. And they've all got their own working dogs here. Unless I can get somebody to take the cottage for eight or nine months who'll take care of him."

"I'll do it," says Aileen. "I'll stay till you get back. I'll take care of him."

Three weeks later Jennifer drives off in her mini for London. She gets twenty miles south and breaks down. She is brought back by the RAC man who seems to like her. He drinks several cups of coffee and finds it difficult to leave, but he does. Jennifer stays the night. The next day the garage brings back her car and off she goes again.

The nights are longer and the days are colder. Aileen phones a number on Jennifer's list for coal. The coalman stands in the kitchen while Aileen counts the money. He is young, his teeth very white when he speaks.

"So Jennifer's gone away for the year and it's you taking care of that old dog," he says. "Jennifer said you were from the North?"

When he is gone Aileen laughs to herself when it comes to her that he has taken with him more information about herself than she remembers giving anyone before. And she has told him something she had not known till now.

He said, "So you'll be away back up North then next July when Jennifer gets back?"

And she said, "No I like it here. I'm going to stay. I'm going to look around for a place of my own when Jennifer does come back."

By the last week of December the farmer is saying it is the worst winter in Drumelzier for a long time. Aileen lines Bob's barrel with extra straw and bags and old blankets. She persuades him one day when the sleet is heavy, horizontal on the wind, to come inside the house, but when she tries to close the door he is anxious and goes out again to his barrel. Then, in the early hours of the first morning of January the sleet stops and, at midday, the sky shows blue through the overcast, then clears. The sun is brilliant on the white fields. Aileen has been five days in the house without a walk.

She sets off along the road but Bob is behind her. She takes him back but he follows her again so she lets him come with her. He is slow at first and veering to the left but he soon warms up and passes her. He is used to being in front. She follows him down across the Iron Bridge, across the Tweed, up and off the main road through Rachan farm and up towards the Dreva Road. They must be three miles from the cottage now and the sky is darkening with snow again. Aileen knows it is time to turn back before the next storm.

But Bob keeps going and does not listen to her shouts. He leaves the road through a break in the dyke and sets off up the hill through the dead bracken towards the old stones standing at the top. Aileen runs to stop him. There is nearly no light left in the sky now. She is slipping in the slush and the mud on the steep hillside. The bracken is trapping her legs and she is soaked when she falls. She cannot catch Bob. She is freezing cold and angry, shouting at him to stop. She feels stupid and useless and afraid. Falling again and again, sometimes almost crawling it is so difficult to climb and the sleet now slashing her face and ears and eyes. She cannot see. She is desperate to catch him, the wind howling down on them both.

The climb and the blizzard are slowing him down now, stopping him. So she catches him amongst the beginning of the high stones, the main fort above them and part of the darkness. She is on her knees crying. He is still looking up towards the top while she holds him, only skin and bone, his ribs almost bursting from the hammering of his heart, his desire to reach the heights that his body cannot match anymore. She puts her face to his coat and shuts her eyes, her tears melting through the ice on his side. There is a warmth between them like a tent, a refuge. And outside the gale and the ghosts are screaming and dancing about them in the chaos.

After a while she lifts her face from his shelter into the cold and the darkness. He turns his eyes from the summit towards her. Watches her.

"Old dog," she says. "Listen. How about this? We'll wait till Spring, till the weather is warm and this hillside is dry and everything is growing green and we'll come up here with some food and we'll sit at the top. We'll have a picnic. We'll lie in the sunshine. But not now. It's the wrong time. Right now I think we should go back. I think we should go home."

So they turn around. They go back down the hill through the storm. They go home together.

Something Else

From Nairn you can see the lighthouse at Tarbet Ness, nineteen miles away across the Moray Firth. Mike MacFarlane had seen its light all his life but he had never been there till he went with Alice Boone and after that he was never there again.

The first time he saw Alice she was serving drink from behind the bar in the Station Hotel in Nairn and doing it very badly.

But Alice had been in there three nights already and no-one seemed to mind when she spilled the drink or dropped the whole glass and shrieked then laughed because they were all laughing with her. It was a Monday night. He'd never seen the place so full or happy.

Usually Mike was not there during the week. It was a Friday or a Saturday when he would come home from the west coast, from Skye, where they were putting up pole lines. Then he was away again by Sunday night. But on the Friday he had stepped backwards into a five foot hole he had just dug. He'd done something to his leg so he was taking the week off.

Alice was red haired, thin, freckles and drama. She would wade into all situations, her arms flailing about her, scattering things that got in the way of her descriptions and explanations, her happiness. She had come from South Lanarkshire and school to the Station Hotel to be a waitress for the summer but the first day she worked J. Johnston had found her too noisy and scary to be with the guests in the dining room. So he put her in the bar where they loved her.

The first time Mike and Alice were out together Alice ate two black pudding suppers, sitting by the sea, the grease dripping down her chin, the thinnest girl he had ever known.

"Generations of deprivation made this appetite", said Alice. "Made these bones."

After the black puddings, the chips, she ate a cake, then chocolate.

So the first time Mike kissed Alice she tasted of all these things, but also fresh, cool, sweet. And because Alice's teeth were, like his, a bit askew, they tapped together like boats moored on evening water.

A week later they went to George Cowie's party on the beach. A fire and drink, July, the sun hardly going down. Alice looked across the water, across the Moray Firth, to the Black Isle.

"What's that light you can see just now and then?" she asked.

"It's the lighthouse," he said. "Tarbet Ness."

"We could go there," she said.

"It's just twenty miles from here across but it's more like sixty by road round the end of the Firth."

"My mother and my father are coming up here on holiday in two weeks," she said. "We could take their car."

Three weeks later they are driving.

But things had happened since the party on the beach.

Mike was back at work in Skye and he was seeing Alice only at weekends. During the week he'd not see her at all then on Friday night when he came home he'd walk in the Station Hotel and he'd see her working, laughing with the customers. George Cowie was always there. He worked in Nairn during the week. The night before Alice and Mike drove to Tarbet Ness Mike had pushed her against a wall. Drunk, jealous, he'd hit her.

They are in the car, Alice driving. On that road the world is a sky full of clouds. But his legs and arms, his head, his face, feel heavy, strange.

Two years later Alice is not flinging her arms about any more. She keeps them close to herself, folded. She does not shriek and laugh any more. She keeps her head down. She does not knock vases and plants and lamps over anymore or enter the room like a flock of seagulls. She is quiet. Watching Mike.

How much he drinks. Now she has a long scar in the white of her eye where he has punched her. Over time he has broken some bones in her face.

At Tarbet Ness they climb down to the beach, the birds screaming, the sea running against the rocks, the shore.

Two years later, in the South on a Sunday morning, Mike wakes and Alice is gone. Maybe she goes away to all the places she does not talk about anymore. Maybe she meets other people, different people. Maybe nowadays she laughs again, spills stuff over her friends, over strangers, crashes into the furniture in people's houses and, with her flying hands, describes in the air the arcs of her tumultuous days and the people who meet her don't mind what she breaks, but laugh instead, because she makes them happy with her shining teeth, her commotion and her red curly hair.

Once he had imagined two people and one of them would be beautiful like Alice and one of them would be himself. Then he met Alice and the situation that he had imagined could have become true. But then it seemed that who he was could not be the other person in this situation, this story. He could not be the person the situation needed to become true because who he was was someone who would destroy it all: Who became crazy and violent with jealousy and rage: Who was outside the situation that he had wanted to be in: Who tried to kill Alice, hating her, condemning her for having seen who he was when he could not be the person that he had imagined he would be in the story: Who destroyed the real story of Alice because of a story that was never true.

After closing time, because JJ's business is failing and Mike has no work to go to any more, and because neither of them has anybody waiting, they clear the tables, they wash up, lock the doors and pour themselves a glass. They put out all the front lights and, carrying the glasses and a bottle each, they go through the back.

They drink into the night, until three, four, five, until they are sure of sleep. Then they leave by the back door, into the last of the night and go separate ways.

And tonight, Winter, through the wind and the rain and the darkness, he can hear, as he walks to his house, the cats screaming and the dogs howling by the river. And he knows whatever he might have been is gone. He knows what he hears out there is not the anguish of animals: There are no animals following him. It is something different. Something else.

Margaret Dewar And Catherine Munro

Sheila Munro and her husband Allan had a baby daughter, Catherine. But six months after the baby was born Sheila died.

Allan Munro tried to carry on with the farm and take care of the baby but, even with the help he got from his relatives and neighbours, he found it hard and both the farm and the baby suffered and did not thrive.

Allan had a neighbour, William Dewar, an old shepherd who was cared for by his daughter Margaret. When William died Allan Munro asked Margaret Dewar to marry him and, although Margaret was forty years old then and Allan much younger, less than thirty, she did. And it was said by people around that of course neither married for love: Allan married to have a mother for his child and a wife for his farm and Margaret Dewar married because she had nursed both her mother and father until they had died and so she was now in the habit of caring for someone and Allan and his daughter were there to be cared for.

But whatever the reasons, and however practical rather than romantic the union, what was extraordinary and marvellous and a revelation to everyone was how much Margaret and the baby Catherine, who was now a year old, loved each other. Right from that very moment these two first saw each other they were happy with each other in a way that was beyond the power of anyone who saw this to describe. From that first time when Margaret had reached out her hand and touched the baby Catherine's hand and the baby Catherine had smiled into Margaret's face, they would spend as many waking hours together as they could find; would collect eggs together, feed chickens together, take Allan's dinner down to the field, cook, clean, wash, go into town together. And each move they made they would talk about, laugh about and consider together.

Then, when she was five, Catherine went to school, two miles down the road. And she would come home after school to Margaret and Margaret would always be there and they would sit at the kitchen table together and talk.

And as Catherine grew and her activities went further and wider, and she went to the secondary school in Nairn, and she was away from Margaret more, wherever she was, when she thought of Margaret, she would stop and look up from whatever she was doing. And Margaret, although she missed Catherine as Catherine's absences grew longer, was happy for her and proud of her and would also now and then, in the midst of her work, stop and shut her eyes and give thanks to God for Catherine, her child, her love, her heart overflowing.

Catherine left Nairn and went to Aberdeen for five years. She came back and she married Billy Riach, a farmer, her boyfriend since school. And when Allan Munro had died and Margaret Munro grew old and the house quiet with no other person living there any more, Margaret sometimes, when she was still, would hear Catherine's voice in the silence. Then she would go and phone Catherine.

But even without this it was always as if they could touch each other over long distances, comfort each other and be with each other no matter what happened. And this was true even after one of them had died and the other was left: In the years remaining to the one who was left there was for her a feeling like a continuous surprise that they had been, in this world that they read about, heard about, the things they had seen, that had happened to themselves, their friends, their neighbours and those about them, so lucky.

Catherine Munro.
Crashing The Car

In 1961, when we were seventeen years old on the farms in Nairnshire, we needed cars because everywhere we wanted to go was twenty or thirty miles away. The cars we got were mostly our father's cars. When evening came we would fill each car with seven or eight of us and away we'd go.

On the farms in Nairnshire then, most of us did not expect to be going away to towns and cities. We expected to live with our parents until we married and maybe even after that. So, after two summers, the cars we borrowed no longer carried a crowd but carried instead only two people. These cars became, while we were in them, our private spaces where we grew up, where we separated ourselves from our parents, where we could leave them behind.

In August 1963, at midnight, Billy Riach and Catherine Munro were driving home the twenty-six miles from the Two Red Shoes in Elgin. They had just come through Forres and had ten miles still to go.

A week after the crash, in the Station Hotel in Nairn, I asked Catherine if Billy had been drinking much that night. She said no, he had not. Maybe one or two. Almost nothing at all. Anyway, she said, the crash had nothing to do with drink. They were right in the middle of harvest, just trying to get home early.

"We were just past Forres," she said. "Before the bridge. I had a packet of cigarettes open in my lap, a cigarette in my mouth, the lighter in my hand. It was a lovely, clear night. A bright moon and dark shadows on the road. Then I saw the strangest thing, the cigarettes rising from the packet and floating around the inside of the car. I tried to catch them.

The next thing seems now, and seemed then, like not just later, or even much later, but instead like a completely different time. I could remember the floating cigarettes very clearly but it was already a memory from another situation altogether. High around me, all around with no trace of a path in, were walls of barley, shining dark yellow in the moonlight.

I was sniffling, like I had been crying in my sleep, and that is how I felt, tired, like you feel after you have been very upset. I kept clicking the lighter, trying to light my cigarette. But it would not light. It seemed very important that I did get it lit and I kept trying and trying even after I knew that the cigarette was broken.

I think I must have been making a lot of noise, crying and swearing, trying to light that cigarette. It was only when I stopped that I could hear, over on my right, a long whine, something away in the distance, a sound like I had never heard before. I walked straight through the barley to the car. The sound was something inside the car, still turning.

Billy was out of the driver's seat with his body across and hiding the steering wheel. His head was through the broken windscreen and his arms were stretched straight out ahead of him as if he had been reaching for something. I stood six feet away. The hard enamel of the car bonnet was liquid around his head. The whine from the car stopped. There was only the sound of the barley and one cry from a nightbird.

I went forward and tried to turn him over. The blood shining in the moonlight confused his features and I did not know where to look into his face. He slipped; back through the windscreen into the car; into the driver's seat. I just stood. I cried and cried. There was nothing else to happen. Perhaps a cloud crossed the moon. We went into darkness.

'Billy! Billy! Billy!' I pulled open his door, shouting at him. 'Look at the car! Look at it! Oh God! Your father's car! What will he say!'

Billy's eyes opened in the blood on his face. I was surprised to see exactly where they were located.

He said, 'Alright. Alright. Alright. I'll try to get it started. Maybe we can drive it back up on the road.'

"And that is what we did," said Catherine. "Drove back up onto the road. But he'll be a month in hospital at least. Cracked his skull but his chest is worse, his ribs completely mangled into him. It'll be a while before he is right again. He'll be okay though. You know what he's like, James? Anyway he's safer in hospital meanwhile. His father is not too pleased about the car. But I'd like another drink. What about yourself?"

She married Billy Riach on September 17th 1969 in the Nairn Old Parish Church at two o'clock.

On the fifteenth of August 1988 I go to the Nairnshire Farmers Show. I am ten feet inside the showfield when I meet John Colquhoun. Together we walk two circuits of the showring. We look at the penned animals, the stalls and W.R.I. tents with the knitting and the cakes. The parades. The descending parachutists. We go slowly. We try to delay going to the beer tents. The previous year John and I, and John's brother Dougie, had gone much too early to the tents. Later in the evening the police had arrested Dougie in the High Street and I had been ill for three days.

This year, when John says, "We'll maybe go and have a look in the tent for Billy Riach," some of the folk have been in there for a very long time. As we step through the flap out of the sunshine I can see Neil Verosky propped against the main tent pole. His eyes are open and he is waving his arms as he speaks but he has been nailed by the collar of his tweed jacket to the wood to keep him up out of the mud.

Billy also has been in the tent for quite a while. But drink these days only makes him look more solid. He cannot, surely, be growing bigger. God. I hope it's not me that's shrunk.

At the back of the tent Catherine is laughing with Lorraine Ross. I shout over, "Hullo Catherine Munro. Hullo Lorraine."

They come over.

Catherine says, "James. James Burns."

She says to Lorraine Ross, "James must be the only person left in the world who still calls me Catherine Munro."

"Maybe he doesn't like changes," says Lorraine Ross.

"I've been married for twenty years," says Catherine. "That's surely long enough for anyone to get used to a change."

Her hair is streaking with grey. The furrows from the corners of her eyes to her jawline are deepening. When she flings back her head and laughs I can see the gold and silver repairs in her teeth. She talks and talks. Arguing. Laughing. I stay listening to her for two hours as we pass each other drink.

I tell her, "Catherine Munro. You are more beautiful every time I see you."

"James Burns," she says. "I hope you are not going to be a nuisance."

An hour later, Billy and I are standing watching two salesmen fighting underneath a trestle table. I say, "Billy, did you ever hear of this thing where people die in an operation or something and they find themselves leaving their bodies and walking up something like a tunnel towards a bright light? They feel really happy and all that but something calls them back and so they don't die but they remember the experience? Did you ever come across anything like that?"

Billy looks at me. "Good God, James. You are getting some very funny ideas down in that Edinburgh place. Maybe it's time you came back home."

We all stay in the tent till the caterers take it down around us. Catherine and I stand at the main gate. The sun is still high, flashing on and off. We watch John Colquhoun and Billy, one on either side and each with an arm of Neil Verosky. John and Billy are pointed South out of the show field and Neil Verosky is struggling North inwards.

Catherine says "God. Farmers. Who would want anything to do with them? Sometimes I wake in the night, crying, like I was still in that barley field and I shake Billy awake and I say to him, 'Billy, you are lucky to be alive.' But all he will ever say is, 'Too true Cath, we're all lucky to be alive'."

"Look at him now," she says.

John and Billy have fallen with Neil at the gate. John and Billy are face down into the mud and Neil is face up looking at the sky.

Catherine laughs and laughs. "Can you believe it? I think we should go off now and just leave them."

And the sun is dropping towards one of those Nairn sunsets, probably honey and wine and wild red golden streaks. Catherine touches my shoulder. She smiles and I want to be here with her forever.

"But I'll tell you this James," she says. "Once I've got him awake, really awake, his eyes open, him sitting up, looking about, I always go to sleep then, no bother."

The Greatest Painter I Ever Knew

In 1998 Matt Weston was made redundant from a job at Bristol Works where, although he was not unhappy, he was only counting down the years.

Now jobless, he felt free to do something he had meant to for a long time. He joined an art class. It was not a very good art class but through it he found a life drawing class that was. The teacher this time was a painter called Chris Cooper.

Matt liked the class and he liked Chris Cooper. In his class he started to know what he wanted to do. His drawing went from being terrible to being less terrible. After the classes some of the students would go with Chris for a drink. Sometimes it was just Chris and Matt. They were both divorced, children grown, no commitments, not even cats or dogs.

Sometime during that first year they became friends. They would go to galleries at weekends, exhibition openings, jazz clubs. They both liked drinking, talking, even a bit of hill walking. By the end of July Matt was going to three of Chris' classes.

Then all the classes stopped for the summer. Matt went down to Cornwall to help his brother-in-law build a house. Chris was also out of Bristol much of the time teaching summer schools. They did not meet again until his classes started again in October.

They went for a drink after the first class of the new session. Chris was quieter than Matt had remembered him. Matt asked Chris what he had done in the summer. Chris said that as well as the summer schools he had gone to a jazz festival in the North of Scotland. Matt said he hadn't realised that Chris liked jazz so much that he would travel so far to hear it. Chris said the festival was great, one of the best going, but that he had also gone hoping to meet someone, a woman, a painter, he had known thirty five years before.

Matt said, "She must have been either a very special woman or a very good painter."

Chris was quiet for a while. Then he said, "She was both. And she was the greatest painter I have ever known. Her name was Catherine Munro."

He said, "In 1965 when I left school in Bristol I wanted to get as far away from home as I could. I went to Art School in Aberdeen. I met Catherine the day we started. We were eighteen years old. But I didn't pay much attention to her then, not for the first four years anyway. Except her work. But everyone noticed her work. Right from the start and no one knew what to make of it. It was realistic but wild. Not like the pop art that was around then though with shades of it. But unfashionable somehow. She painted mostly in oils but used other materials as well. She painted tenements, streets, skies, people, landscapes, the sea, storms, rain, stuff from her kitchen, almost anything, but extraordinary.

I remember one, I remember them all, but one especially, a painting of a pram at the back of a tenement, the wheels like mandalas, grounded but floating, the odd colours, disconcerting, beautiful. The first time I saw it I was shocked. Disturbed. I never knew a painting like that could exist. I never knew painting could do that. Could be that good. That different.

And Catherine herself was outside things. As a person. Everyone knew her work was good but at the same time it was like they suspected their own judgement. And Catherine. Like there was some kind of irregularity no one could quite define. Grasp. As if Catherine herself was some kind of irregularity, some deviant not included in our idea of things or how we wanted things to be. She even looked separate. Odd. She wore these faded blue cut off boiler suits of her father's. He was a farmer. The boiler suits were practical, the way she sloshed paint around, but too big for her. She was small. Sturdy. She had short brown curly hair, freckles and very red cheeks like she had just come in from the cold. As well she was always blushing: Deep red with excitement or embarrassment and especially when she talked or worked. And in drawing classes you could hear her breathing like she was running a marathon. Well, I suppose she was. Whenever she came out with us for a drink, which was not often because she was never part of any crowd, she would get drunk very easily and talk wildly about art, history, farming, dogs, anything. Politics. In the bars she would talk to anyone; old men, sailors down the harbour. Once she got going you could never get her to stop. She was exhausting, and always in terrible clothes but not in an art school way: Like she'd been dressed by her grandmother then fallen off a bike several times. She was just odd. I think we were mostly embarrassed to be with her. She was too much for us. Too enthusiastic. Definitely not cool.

It was not until after four years, when we both got a post diploma, an extra year, and we had to share a studio, that I had much to do with her. I was surprised. She was easy to share with. Easy to work with. She had long stopped trying to socialise with the crowd. Not that she'd ever tried that hard. I don't know what she did when she wasn't working. I think she went home North most weekends.

In the studio we would start the morning early with coffee together. At night take the same bus into town. Or walk. We were always talking except when we were working. Then she was very quiet. Except for the breathing. I don't know. Which I quite liked. She made me laugh.

I had a girlfriend Alison. She was in her fourth year doing jewellery. We'd been living together for two years. We looked good together. We were always at anything going on. I fell for her the first time I saw her. She was very beautiful. She still is.

Anyway, I really got to like Catherine. She had a boyfriend

up North. A farmer. I only met him once. I don't think he came to Aberdeen often. I suppose that's why Catherine went back home at weekends. I don't think he liked cities. Catherine didn't say much about him. I can't remember much anyway. I can't remember his name.

My friends were curious about Catherine and I sharing a studio. I don't know what they had expected but they seemed surprised we got on so well. I didn't talk a lot about it. I think I had become defensive about Catherine. They would tease me saying, 'How's your crazy pal?'

Alison would say, 'It must be difficult being stuck with her in that room all day.'

And I would reply, 'No, it's ok. Catherine's fine.'

And she was. She helped me with my work somehow. Not directly. She wasn't analytical or critical. I think it was just her attitude to work. Her relationship to paint. She just painted. She just kept going till she could see something. She would take her drawing and set forth upon a board or canvas and if the painting did not work out, did not seem to be going anywhere she wanted it to go, she did not hesitate to paint over it, over the hours and hours of work, start again. She said you need a good four or five layers underneath just to get going. At least one of her paintings I knew had fifteen layers at least. Sometimes she kept painting on the canvas until the canvas and stretcher were wrecked. She was better on board; it fought back. And she was very good humoured. She was never discouraged when things did not work out, she just started again.

Catherine and I both applied to go to the Royal College in London at the end of our time in Aberdeen. This would give us another three years studio time. We talked a lot about it.

'Keep us away from the real world for as long as possible,' Catherine said.

After the final shows in July, (Catherine's show was just great, stunning, more than even I, who had been seeing her paintings for five years, watching them grow from their beginnings, could have imagined) before we all went away for the summer, and some of us for good, we had a big party, lots of people in a big house near Union Street: Lots of drink and everybody going wild after all the tension, the work, the exposure of the shows: Folk all over the place yelling and dancing, weeping and being sick. All these things going on. I hadn't drunk so much myself. Alison and I had gone out for a meal with her mother and father who had come up to see her show. We came late to the party.

Alison and I did not stick together much at these things. I wandered about being hugged or shouted at above the din but still feeling a bit detached as you do when most people are drunker than you are. Then I found Catherine.

She was sitting on this sofa that could have held five people but just then only her. I sat beside her. She was wearing a white shirt, denim skirt and sandals. For Catherine she was very dressed up. We talked a bit. Just chat. I don't know.

I'll tell you this, and I don't know when I first realised this, when I first knew it, but I did know it, only I didn't think about it if you know what I mean, but whenever I met Catherine anywhere lately I would feel as if I had arrived. Like at this party, I don't think I was looking for her, in fact I hadn't expected her to be there, it was just that when I found her I felt I did not need to wander about anymore. I had got to wherever I was going.

Also lately I had been irritated with my friends and even with Alison but I thought that this would pass once all the worry of getting my show up was over. The last few weeks I had just wanted to get back to the studio where I worked and where Catherine was always working, so when I found her at the party it was fine. I felt relaxed just sitting there with her. I had the feeling we were very still, an island in all the chaos. Just sitting together on the sofa. We had stopped talking, just watching people dancing, falling about. Then Catherine said something like 'so are you alright?' Just a question. Then we were looking at each other. We hadn't been but had been looking round the room as we spoke, side by side. Then the short silence. Then Catherine spoke. Then we were looking at each other.

I don't think we had ever looked at each other before. Not really. Not into each other's faces. It was like a shock. It was a shock. It was like you have been walking down a stair in the dark and you think you have reached the last step, the level, and you put your foot out and it was not the last step, there is another one and your whole body goes into this shock, especially in your chest. My heart. I lost my breath. Or stopped breathing anyway. At the same time some emotion like blood was swelling in my throat, my face. I could not believe what was happening or had already happened. Maybe when people get killed they feel like this. Everything outside us in the room seemed to go on, real and normal, but not us. Like we had lost gravity. She was so beautiful. She was so beautiful and I loved her so much and I couldn't, I don't know, I couldn't something whatever it was, anything, function maybe. I remember I had a separate thought like a panic thinking I'd never be able to do anything ordinary ever again, I had just lost my world. I loved her and it was going deeper all the time or had been deep and was now drowning me. She was looking at me, her eyes all bright, her too, and her mouth slightly open (I could see the tips of her teeth) as if she might speak but she didn't and I could hear her breathing in our worlds stopped while the rest, everything else, carried on.

Then some of the dancers fell on us. Somebody pulled or pushed me off the sofa, laughing, wanting me to dance, all these people between us.

So I was hauled away still disorientated. Useless with emotion. The muscles in my face trembling. All these people around. Then Alison was there. Somebody giving me an address, wanting mine. All these things going on. It seemed a long time before I could get back to where Catherine had been. She wasn't there. I looked through the whole house. Outside.

Everywhere. But she was gone.

But it was alright. I was kind of relieved at the respite. I was desperate to see her but also glad, though not totally glad, anxious glad, tense glad, to be able to go on as if I was the same, as if everything was normal. I should have gone after her but I carried on with the party. I don't know. These were my friends. There was Alison. It is difficult to just walk out and I didn't know time was critical. My heart was hammering for hours but I thought I needed to act calmly.

Even when I went into the Art School the next day and did not see Catherine but saw all her stuff gone, even then I felt fine. I still thought we had plenty of time. I had woken wondering if the whole thing had happened. Hoping it hadn't, hoping it had. When I didn't see Catherine I wanted to see her but I was glad of the delay. It was all so scary. I had a hole in my chest from wanting to see her but I wanted time to get hold of myself again.

Even when I heard that she had already left Aberdeen it seemed ok. We would be together in London for three years, forever, where we could work it out.

I began to feel as if I needed the summer.

I could have got Catherine's home address then, or her telephone number. Somebody would have had them, but I did not know what to say to her or want to pursue her up North where I had never been. I did not know what kind of situation I might find myself in up there on the farms: Wild fellows with shotguns maybe who were not pleased to see me.

So I went home to Bristol to work for the summer. I phoned the Art School and they said they would forward any letters I wrote to Catherine. Then after about four weeks Catherine wrote and said that she would not be coming to the Royal College in London after all: She was going to marry her farmer boyfriend: She wished me lots of luck and success: She signed the letter, Love Catherine.

I did go to the Royal College. I started, but I had some kind of breakdown. It took me a year and a half to get going again. Alison was also in London. She was great, very good to me at the worst times.

Eventually I started again at the Royal College. I did ok. Alison and I married and we had, we have two children, Beth and David. Alison and I separated when they were eight and ten. Alison met someone else and she is married again. I see her and her husband and it's alright. She seems happy.

Even before I finished the Royal College I realised that I had only an average talent as a painter. It was fashion that had taken me so far. But during my breakdown I discovered in hospital that I loved to teach. Working in the art room with the other patients I found that seeing other people's work, the surprises, seeing it develop, (like yours) was better than being with my own, or in fact fed my own. Made things worthwhile. Gave me direction. That art was clearer to me, more exciting, watching it evolve in the hands of someone else.

After London and the Royal College an old friend told me about a job here in Bristol. I came home and here I am."

"So what happened during the summer?" Matt asked.

"Well, at the summer school, one of the students, we were talking about jazz, he said he had been to a Jazz Festival the previous summer in the North of Scotland, at a place called Nairn. Nairn is where Catherine came from. Or near.

Now in all the thirty five years since I had last seen Catherine I had thought about her every day. At first it had been very difficult, torture, to think of her and at other times I'd almost forget, remember her more gently. Eventually, especially after I was divorced, it became different, like a warmth, just part of me. I think that knowing Catherine's extraordinary talent I had assumed that sooner or later I would see her work or hear of her and her work somewhere. But I never did. In all that time, nothing. No one I knew ever heard anything about her.

So I decided to go to Nairn. But I did not work it out very

well. I should have got in touch with Catherine in some kind of way before I ever went, but after I had decided to go things got very confused. Difficult. In my mind. I felt a bit of what I did all those years ago at the time of my breakdown. So when the time of the Festival came I just got in my car and drove the five hundred miles, more, to Nairn.

I booked into a bed and breakfast near the centre of the town. The jazz itself, each performance I had come to see, was outstanding. Great concerts. Great atmosphere. The music perfect for how I was. For anytime. But I became more and more worried I might meet Catherine by accident and I could find no way to tell her I was there. The people in the bed and breakfast had only been in Nairn three years and I didn't know Catherine's married name. I couldn't just ask anybody if they knew her, I was worried they would turn out to be a relative, someone who would lead me straight to her which would be all wrong or tell her about me and she'd be worried. I felt like a stalker. I kept hearing her voice all the time in the local accent. I only felt safe when I was in a concert. Not even then really.

Also I was worrying about my daughter Beth. She and her husband, who I had never found an easy man to get along with, have had a few problems lately. I spoke to her before I went North but she said I should go. From Nairn I phoned her but I got no answer. I phoned David but he said not to worry, they'd maybe just gone away for a few days together to work things out. But I was worrying about her all the time when I was not worrying about meeting Catherine. I wanted to be where Beth could find me if she needed me like I'd always been before.

So when the last performance finished I drove through the night back to Bristol. Eleven hours, all wrong. I was stopping in lay-bys beating my head with my fists. Kneeling in the mud and rubbish howling, crazy, what a mess. The police stopped. Said was I ok? Said they hoped I'd do nothing foolish. I told them that anything foolish I could think of, I'd already done. But they made me feel better somehow. Their young faces. I wanted to behave better in front of them. Saner. So I got back in the car and drove home.

And Beth is fine. She and her husband are doing ok. He's alright really. He seems to love her anyway. And she can be a bit fierce herself."

"So that's it? That's it all over? Catherine Munro?" said Matt.

"No, no," said Chris. "No. Not at all. I just need to do everything the right way this time. I need to think about things. Be kind of sane about it all. I'll write Catherine so she knows I still exist. If she remembers me. I'll address the letter with what I know. The Post Office in Nairn will deliver it. Work it out if they can. I'm sure they'll be able to. I'll ask her how she is, how her painting is. I'll tell what I'm doing. See what her situation is. Just see what happens. Whatever she wants. It would be good to see her again, even to speak to her on the phone. We'll see, just see. So that's it. That's it so far. It's going to be ok. So do you want another drink?"

"OK, Great," Matt said. "But it's my turn. I'll get them."

So he did. There was a good band that night. There was time for a couple more.

After Matt and his first wife, Lilian, had been long divorced he worked with a man called Hodges who had known Lilian's family before Matt did. Hodges showed Matt a photograph of Lilian and her two sisters on a beach in Cornwall. This photograph had been taken the summer Lilian and Matt had first met: Maybe just weeks or even days before they met.

When Matt saw this photograph he had a terrible shock. He fell in love with the girl in the photograph while at the same time he knew he had already lost her. His whole life, that had seemed alright until then, went completely wrong in that instant.

After this, for many months, Matt was very depressed. Very lost. Everything seemed pointless. Meaningless. He felt that his life was a failure. He felt without any hope. He had looked at

Lilian in that photograph, laughing with her sisters, and he was afflicted by a terrible despair about the future, her future, their future, that he already knew, that was already his past but that the Lilian in the photograph did not yet know.

Yet Lilian and Matt had never been deeply attached and their separation (and eventual divorce) was a relief to them both.

But what happened to Matt when he saw that photograph was the worst thing he had ever known. The months after were awful. What he saw in that photograph was, somehow, his own death.

Matt knows this is nothing like the story Chris Cooper told. He knows the two stories are not the same. Only that when Chris told Matt about Catherine Munro, Matt remembered the time after he had seen Lilian's photograph and he wanted to tell Chris about it. But instead he got them both another drink and talked about other things. So he has never said anything. Not yet anyway.

Catherine And The Colours In The Sky

When Billy is more than two hours late Catherine goes up the hill to look for him. She finds him on the North side with the collie, Oakley, lying near him, keeping the crows from his eyes. Billy is on the step dug by the sheep into the hillside, fallen or lain back from where he had been sitting. His hands are on his chest, right over left, his fingers extended as if he is showing her where the trouble is. Or had been. There is no trouble now.

Catherine sits beside him, too late for any hurry. Billy had lived much longer than they had ever expected, hauling his wrecked chest through forty winters. Now this is the end of summer and he has died in a place he would have called good, only the sky over him, the farmlands and the sea below.

And today the sky is beautiful. You can see one hundred miles and beyond into the North. A jade blue sky streaking with pink. Light greens and yellows line the horizon. Down at the house Catherine has four boards, four feet by six feet, their surfaces worked on for weeks already, stained, scraped, textured. She is working on them all together; switching back and forth like a slow motion drummer whenever she is lost or hesitant on one. This sky overhead is perfect, the colours she needs next.

She feels the cold coming in. The sun going down in an hour. She'd better get to the house. Call whoever you call. Call Margaret, she will know what to do. And the children, though hardly children anymore, tell them their father is dead.

The sky is softening now, the light going. Once, years before, driving West back from Aberdeen, she had seen two huge pillars of cloud before her, glowing red and miles high, people stopping in lay-bys, the light so strange, and she had stopped too and watched for forty minutes this sun go down. She had thought then, standing there, how it would be to keep going, to keep driving west into the clouds as they disappeared into the night. So that is how she had tried to paint them. Waiting. Like some giant fading gate.

A painting still not finished. Still not worked out. Not yet.

She stands. Oakley looks awkward but determined as if Catherine might ask her to come down the hill. She wants to stay with Billy.

"It's alright," says Catherine. "it's alright, Oakley. You stay with him till I come back. Keep those crows away. Good girl."

Catherine leaves Billy and the dog. Yesterday if she'd come up here with Billy they'd have walked down home together, talking, arguing, laughing, the day going, the darkness coming over them till they can hardly see each other anymore, only the lights of the towns far below out there on the coast.

Anthroposophists In Love

On his twenty-sixth birthday James comes running down Gilmore Park from the canal and trips over an extending dog lead that is stretched across the pavement outside the Fingertips Sauna and Angel Model Agency.

James is badly injured in the fall. The palms of both his hands are scraped raw and bloody, his chin and knees feel broken or at least cracked. He manages to stand up, dizzy with pain, but he does not shout, Good God, are you trying to kill me. Perhaps he is in shock, although later he will always insist that it is in this instant, as he tries to focus his eyes, that he falls in love.

On one end of the long dog lead is the ugliest dog that James has ever seen and on the other is a woman so beautiful that James, at first, cannot speak.

This woman has dark hair pulled with a scarf into a pleat down her back. She has small dark eyes and a large wide mouth set in stern disapproving lines. Her clothes are like those of a school mistress in an early John Wayne western and she is holding a large book.

She says, "Why must you rush about so dangerously and madly? Why cannot you walk peaceably and calmly?"

James says, "Sorry."

He feels faint and he knows he is losing blood from somewhere.

He says, "What a beautiful dog you have. What is his name?"

The woman says, "He is not a beautiful dog and I do not have him. He is probably the ugliest dog in the world. He is my sister's dog but she has gone to California and she has not come back. I do not like dogs but I am meanwhile stuck with him. His name is Euripedes."

Euripedes sits down and leans against the wall of the Scottish and Newcastle Brewery. He has the body of a greyhound, only very hairy with black, brown, white and rust coloured irregular tufts, and the face of a bulldog, but with long spaniel ears. The woman tugs at the lead and she and Euripedes set off up Gilmore Park towards the canal. James limps along beside her.

James says, "What is your book about?"

She says, "It is about re-incarnation."

"No kidding," says James, "Are you a Buddhist?"

"No," she says, "I am an Anthroposophist."

"Great," says James. "That's really great. I'd like to know more about that."

The woman looks at James. She is very cautious. She says, "If you are really interested there is a public talk on Friday night. You could go to that if you want."

"Smashing," says James. "You tell me where it is. I'll meet you at the door. What's your name?"

For the last three years James has been living on Yeaman Place. He works at home in his flat carving wooden decoy ducks for a man called MacLeish MacLeish. MacLeish MacLeish is the most famous decoy duck maker in the world. He is so famous that he has no time to make decoy ducks because he spends all his time opening exhibitions and lecturing in America. Although James makes the wooden ducks, he does not like them. The ducks, designed by MacLeish MacLeish, are sweet, coy and cuddly, but James knows that real ducks are amongst the worlds most dangerous creatures. Real ducks are swaggeringly arrogant, self-confident and megalomaniacal. They fight all day and, in the springtime, the exuberance of their mating (and this always on the canal from midnight till 4a.m.) has kept the residents of Yeaman Place awake for weeks of nights and one year the exertions of these ducks raised such waves that the water burst the canal banks and flooded the houses on the north-west side. James despises the wooden whimsies of MacLeish MacLeish and he dreams that one day he will reveal to the world the true nature of ducks.

After the lecture on Friday night, James and Anna-Marie are walking home.

"Ooooooooh!" Anna-Marie is moaning. "I have never been so ashamed in my life. How could you do it? I can never face my friends or appear at the Anthroposophical Society ever again."

"Och," says James. "How was I to know? The man asked if there were any questions. I bet there were lots of folk listening who wondered if we could be reincarnated as ducks."

Fourteen years later, on midsummers day, James and Euripedes are sitting on Arthurs Seat where the earth had heaved and burst and is now paused in this 350 million year old gesture. Edinburgh and her other six hills are around and below them. To the North is the Forth Rail Bridge and the Road Bridge to Nairnshire, to Lethen. The midsummer beacons burn in the hills. James does not work for MacLeish MacLeish any more. Instead he makes furniture which he takes to London and sells. Euripedes is now a very old dog. He cannot stand up without James' help but once on his feet he can walk stiffly and slowly for very long distances. Anne-Marie is over in Switzerland at a conference. She spends less and less time with James and Euripedes.

James says to Euripedes, "It is like the first rockets on a spaceship that get it off the ground into space and beyond earth's gravity. When the spaceship is free these first rockets are empty and drop away. That's what Anna-Marie did for us. She was there to get us into Anthroposophy and now we don't need her anymore."

James thinks of Anna-Marie over in Dornach talking to tall Germans with big white teeth who have read all one million pages of Steiner's works.

"Do you ever feel, Euripedes," asks James, "that your heart is breaking?"

He starts to read again from The Philosophy of Freedom. "I am on page one hundred and twenty eight, Euripedes. With this, and the ninety-one pages I have read from The Knowledge of Higher Worlds, we have only another nine hundred and ninety-nine thousand, seven hundred and eighty-one pages to go. But not much about dogs yet. Not so far anyway."

Two summers later, Euripedes dies. James wraps him in a MacArthur plaid and carries him up Arthurs Seat in the darkness. James buries Euripedes near the top.

Anna-Marie sends James a postcard from South America. She says, "The heat of the world comes up from the earth through the soles of my feet. I will never leave this place."

Nowadays, James notices that Arthurs Seat is changing shape. Whenever he has been away from Edinburgh and is arriving back again, he can see, waiting for him, raised in volcanic stone high above the city, the shape of a very big, very ugly, very old dog.

Anthropsophists In Love. Part Two. Rain

One very close Summer’s night James was mugged as he came round the corner from St. Peter's Place onto Dundee Street. He saw the Scottish and Newcastle digital clock above the road change from 8.35 to 27oC before youths clad in nursery colours knocked him unconscious to the ground.

James hardly saw his attackers. Perhaps they were not youths at all. Perhaps they were old age pensioners, disguised in anoraks, forced into crime by the Poll Tax. But the experience of the human race since time itself began told James that whoever knocks you over the head in the street is most likely a young male.

James woke in a yellow ward. A large nurse with blonde streaked brown hair and turquoise gold eye shadow was busy on his right. Sunlight striped her white uniform. She saw James open his eyes.

"So you're awake," she said. "And for God's sake don't say where am I? I mean, don't try to speak at all. I'll answer all your questions without you ever even asking. My name is Nurse Murray. You are in Ward three, the male suicide ward. We know now that you did not try to commit suicide. A week after you were brought in witnesses told us you were mugged. God knows why they waited a week. Until then we thought you'd jumped off the Brewery wall, though it's only eight feet high. Then the doctors decided we'd better leave you in here. There was no point in shifting you around with you all wired up like that. Also there is no one else in here anyway because of the World Cup. Though God knows we will be crowded enough if Scotland lose tomorrow night. The reason you can't speak is because your jaw is broken badly along with other things. You have been unconscious for two weeks. You've not missed any good news. If you want to see the television you'll have to wait till you can walk, which might be quite a while. If you need anything just you ring that bell and maybe somebody will come but it will not be me because I've done my bit and I'm going home."

Three days later she said, "And since you don't ask, I'll tell you. I don't like being a nurse. How would you like a job where everyone you meet has just had bad luck? Do you think hospitals are full of lucky people? I'll tell you something. Two years ago they published this survey of every city in Britain and do you know the city where people were the least likely to get mugged? Edinburgh! Glasgow was twelfth and London was eighty sixth. That makes you very special. That makes you very unusual. You have been mugged in the city where it is least likely anybody could be mugged. So you cannot call yourself lucky and I am not in a job where I can congratulate people on their good luck however temporary that good luck might have turned out to be and in my experience good luck is always short lived."

James lay on the white sheets. He had once worked with a man called Jim. Jim had said to James that what happened to you was a kind of choice you made. James hoped that with this spare time here he would be able to meditate on what Jim had said and on it's connection with James being mugged. James hoped this. He also knew he would not. James knew that the best he could expect from this situation philosophically was a state of bafflement. Bafflement was the only reliable finale to any event that James had ever experienced. James had an Uncle John in Skye. Uncle John had said to James, "Always row your boat out into the fog, son. If you wait for the fog to clear before you go fishing you'll starve to death."

James sweated through the long hospital nights. The old dog Euripedes had been dead for five years. Twelve months ago

James was still walking on the canal path at seven thirty each morning as he had done when Euripedes was alive. He had begun to notice a woman in a black fringed leather jacket and black Doctor Marten boots walking a cream coloured dark faced Bull Mastiff dog past where James rested on the concrete slab opposite Caledonia Works. He knew he was in love. The Bull Mastiff had that blank look that large pedigree dogs and male middle-aged joggers have. The woman kept her head down, looking at the mud and litter on the canal bank. James fell in love with the top of her head, her leather fringes and her boots.

One morning, after four days planning and a careful choice of words, he called, "Good morning," as she passed.

She stopped. She looked at him. She said, "Listen son. I've just woke up. And so has this dog. Neither of us has eaten yet. This dog looks at me and he sees someone he trusts and adores. He looks at you and he sees breakfast. So you keep your observations on the morning to yourself and I'll keep mine to myself."

The next day James, sitting by the canal at 7.30 a.m. knew with relief that he had fallen out of love already. The regrets he felt were for the dog. To Harrison Park and back was too short a walk for a Bull Mastiff. He had already seen himself and the creature loping together as far as Colinton, even Balerno, while the rosy fingers of dawn tentatively touched the steam shrouded columns of the Scottish and Newcastle.

James left the Royal Infirmary on a Wednesday.

The golden nurse said, "I'll just see you to the door."

She was wearing long earrings, each made of four golden shells.

At the door she said, "We have had three months together and you unable to say a word. Do you think I will ever hear you speak and would you even recognise me in ordinary clothes? Perhaps good relationships can be based on change and insecurity but I don't believe it. My first name is Rain. I was christened Elaine but I had a little sister who could not say Elaine and so she called me Rain. Your taxi is here. Now I shall wave you away like a brief encounter."

James got in the taxi. The driver had a long pony tail tied with a purple ribbon. He looked round. His face was lined and his hair was going grey.

He said, "Where to?"

James handed him a note: 'The Dog and Cat Home, Portobello.'

The taxi driver said, "I had a great dog once. She died of old age at fifteen. Fifteen! What can you do? They break your heart."

Out of the back window James could see the golden nurse waving. He could not believe he would never see her again. But he knew he did not want to get mugged again. Especially in Edinburgh, a city that had always been good to him. He did not want to cause it to slip from the number one position of non-mugging cities. He knew there were easier ways to meet people. He also knew there were ways to find a dog other than falling in love with its owner. Rain Murray did not have a dog and James felt this made his feelings for her more reliable.

Seventeen years ago James had first loved Anna-Marie. She had left him with her dog Euripides. He was a dog sitter for the ugliest dog in Scotland for twelve years. James and Euripides had waited together for Anna-Marie. They watched the seasons change and pass. They had seen Arthurs Seat white with snow. They had climbed through the ashes together when it was burnt and charred in one summer’s drought. When Euripides died, for James the seasons ended. He did not care if Anna-Marie came back or not.

The taxi arrived outside the gate of the Dog and Cat Home. James gave the driver four pounds fifty. The taxi driver said, "Human beings live for seventy years, dogs live for fifteen years. Maybe that is the nature of love."

James stands at the gate of the Dog and Cat Home. In half an hour he will come out with a dog. This dog might one day bite his neighbour's children, or run in front of a car and cause a terrible crash. It might find him frozen and nearly dead in a snow drift and save his life. It might pull him and many others from a burning house. Or maybe none of these things.

In the office, Mrs. Johnston says to James, "Sign here. Dogs are not like people. People spend their lives hoping for good things and trying to avoid bad things. We try to get a better grip on it all as we get older. At the end we hope to be neither too sad nor afraid. Dogs are different. When dogs get near the end their bodies shrink to skin and bones and their eyes fill with dreams. Elspeth will take you over to the kennels and you can look for your dog."

Elspeth leads James across the tarmac westwards. Seagulls are screaming in the windlessness and the Firth of Forth is still and blue. Inside the walls every dog in the world is barking. Elspeth unlocks the door. In James goes.

All The Roads To Your Door

Seven years after they were divorced Les' ex-wife Angie moved forty miles from Edinburgh into South Lanarkshire to a house beside a railway on a farm above a river.

At first, because there was a lot of work to do to the house, Les would take their two boys (who stayed with Les during the week) down on a Friday night and the three of them would stay there with Angie till the Sunday night or Monday morning, Les and Angie working on the house.

But Les staying there two or three nights a week with Angie started to affect their divorce, which had been very successful up until then. All their agreements and organisation started to fall apart and this was bad for their two boys, bad for them all, so eventually Les did not stay there over-night anymore. Instead he would drive the boys down to Angie's house on a Friday night, return to Edinburgh, then go back and collect them on Sunday afternoon.

So that's how it was that on Sunday afternoons Les would be driving down the A702 on his own, no one else in the car, and any hitchhikers he saw he gave them a lift, usually to the M74 motorway South just two miles from Angie's house.

But this time, in early summer, Les had not seen any hitchhikers until he was nearly at Angie's house, about seven miles still to go. Then, two miles after Biggar, slowing to go round the right angled bend at the far end of the village of Coulter, Les saw a hitchhiker, a dark-headed, white-faced, dishevelled fellow carrying a plastic shopping bag.

And on Friday and Saturday nights the young farm workers, the shepherds and country boys of South Lanarkshire, head into the towns, into Biggar, and drink and eventually maybe fall down and sleep then wake up hours later in some unusual place. The next day you might see them in the morning, or even afternoon, very sick looking, on the A702 or other roads, walking home.

So when he pulled the car in at Coulter and waited for the hitchhiker to catch up, Les thought this might be one of the farm boys just trying to get home.

But straightaway, as soon as the hitchhiker came to the window of the car and Les said,

"Where are you going?"

And the hitchhiker said "Birmingham."

Les could see this was no country boy; stark white hands and not as young as Les had first thought him to be. In his hair and on his clothes bits of grass and smudged earth, his eyes poor, red bloodshot and sore.

Les said, "I'll take you to the motorway. That'll take you South."

And the hitchhiker said, "Great, great, thank you."

Les pulled out on the road again.

"So, what are you going to Birmingham for?"

"Because God has told me to go," said the hitchhiker.

So Les said "Right," and drove on for a mile.

Then said, "How does God do that?"

So the hitchhiker told Les that every now and then God would tell him to get the map, look at it spread out, and God would tell him where to go this time. Then the hitchhiker would go to where God had shown him and preach there. He would just arrive at the place and go to an open public area and start to preach about God. And he never had to carry, or worry about, food or money or where to stay because Christian people, or even others, would take him home and feed him and give him somewhere to stay while he was in that town; preaching every day until God told him it was enough, it was time to go home.

The hitchhiker told Les this time he had been very slow on the journey. He had left Edinburgh on Saturday morning and he was now only 30 miles South by Sunday afternoon. Les asked him where he had stayed on Saturday night. The hitchhiker said that on Saturday evening he had reached Biggar and had walked out of the town till it was nearly dark and still no lift. He was very tired so he had climbed a dry-stone dyke and lain down at the edge of the field and slept.

In the morning when he woke he could not open his eyes. They were glued shut. But he could see the red light of the sun through his eyelids and feel its heat on his face so he knew it was day.

"Good God," said Les, "I mean, sorry, I mean what did you do?"

The hitchhiker said, "I got down on my knees and thanked God for making me blind. Well not blind but kind of blind, a bit like Paul. I asked God what he would like me to do."

Les said, "So what happened? What did God say? What did he want you to do?"

The hitchhiker said that after a while one of his eyes became a bit less glued shut and he could see very slightly out of the little gap. Then he heard church bells so he walked back into Biggar to the church. The bells stopped before he got there but he found the church. The service had already started nevertheless he went in. After the service was over the congregation gave him tea and biscuits. His eyes were still a bit itchy, sore and swollen, but he could see well enough, so he set off again South.

Les said, "See that field you slept in last night, what was in it? Was it yellow?"

The hitchhiker said, "Yes. Yes it was. Yellow, like gold."

"Well," said Les, "It was stuff called rape. Rape Seed. You are allergic to it. It's given you a kind of hayfever. It's affected your eyes. That's what happened to you. You should try to stay clear of it from now on."

The hitchhiker said, "That's amazing. That you should come along and know this. That God has given you this knowledge and that we should meet and that you can explain what happened to me."

Les said he was surprised that no-one in the church had explained it. But then maybe they had been a bit taken aback when a man covered in dry grass and earth and bits of weeds and plants came staggering into church, his face swollen and hair awry, bumping and groping his way down the pews: Maybe a bit of a shock for them.

The hitchhiker said they had all been very good and kind people.

At the roundabout that leads onto the M74 motorway Les said the hitchhiker should go into the motorway services and use the toilets for a tidy up, pick the grass out of his hair, brush himself down, then he might get lifts easier. Les bought some sandwiches and juice. He gave them to the hitchhiker and the hitchhiker said God bless you and Les left him there and went back along the 702 to Angie's house.

When Les arrives at Angie's house in the summer and the day is warm sometimes she is lying in the sun. Maybe the boys are down at the river. When she sees him arrive she raises herself onto her elbows as he parks the car, or sits up and draws her knees to her chin as he walks down towards her. Or she might get up and walk to her house, her right hand pushing her hair from her eyes where it falls again straightaway. Or she might stop on the way to the house to look about her in that dreamy way she has in the sun. Or she might offer Les coffee and go into the house and forget to make it till he goes in the house and makes it for them both. She is always, when he finds her, looking into some distance, Angie, beyond Les or the house or the garden or even the sky. Les does not know where she is looking, but it is not now, nor has it been for a long time, at him any more.

In the first century, after the crucifixion of Christ, Saul (known later as Paul) a persecutor of Christians (he had watched and approved of the stoning to death of Stephen) was blinded on his way to hunt down Christians in Damascus. He was led into the city and lay there for three days. Then Christ spoke to Ananais, a devout follower of Christ. Christ told Ananais that he was to go to Saul, that Saul had already been told by Christ that Ananais was going to come.

Ananais must have been very shocked and frightened by what Christ said, what Christ was asking him to do, and that Christ had already told Saul Ananais' name, because Ananais knew that Saul had come to Damascus to search for the followers of Christ, to imprison and to kill them.

But Christ had not left Ananais much option: Ananais could go on the run from Saul but not from Christ (or from himself). Or could he go and see Saul and take the chance that Christ knew what he was doing. But Ananais was very doubtful about the whole thing and he pointed this out to Christ. But Christ just said go and do it, so Ananais did.

And it seemed to have worked out. Saul got his sight back and began preaching enthusiastically about Christ and the gospel, and preparing folk for the apocalypse. And Ananais was alright, that time anyway, but as he is never mentioned again in any of the testaments we don't know anything more about him or what happened to him.

Nor did Les ever know what happened to the hitchhiker. But he thinks about him. Especially sometimes.

In the new year of 1998, on Sunday afternoon just as it is getting dark, Angie phones Les. He is due to start work at nine o'clock the next day. But Angie says she needs to go South to Bristol to see her father and mother. Les says he will take her. It is a seven hundred and fifty mile round trip but Les reckons he can make it back North in time to start work if they leave now. The boys stay with Angie's sister. Les drives South from Edinburgh and collects Angie from her house. They set off in the darkness and wind and sleet now started though the weather earlier that day had been alright.

It is a fearsome journey, driving almost blind, the windscreen wipers going full speed all the way, into the sleet now turned hammering rain and insane monster clouds of spray in the wakes of the lorries. They stop only once, disorientated, out of the darkness into the bright spaces and coloured lights, machines and hamburgers of the motorway rest.

Les goes to the toilet, Angie for coffee. Coming back he sees her, sixty feet away, through the layers of misted glass, the noise of children and distracted people, bleeping games, crashing dishes. She is sitting holding but not drinking her coffee, looking out into the night. He goes to her, her tired beautiful face turning towards him. He sits with her. Drinks the coffee.

After a while she touches his hand. "We'd better go".

They go back out onto the M6.

At midnight, after a cup of tea with Angie's mother and father, Les leaves Bristol and Angie in the house where she was a child and heads North into the weather no better, even worse, driving all night till he crosses the border back into Scotland, into sleet again, an icy continuous blizzard. He is following the wheel tracks of the lorries who go before him, the actual location of the road itself becoming less and less clear.

At exit 13 Les leaves the lorries and drives off the motorway onto the 702, only an hour now (he thinks) from home. He has been smelling oil for some time but he had thought it was from the lorries. He stops in a lay-by and pulls the bonnet release lever. He gets out into the storm, lifts the bonnet and the whole engine is suddenly on fire. He falls back. Then he starts throwing slushy snow on the blaze. With this, and the continuous sleet, eventually there is just smoke, the whole engine and bonnet black with soot and oil and everything burnt looking. He is in the blackness of the night and the whiteness of the blizzard, soaking, freezing, dirty and despairing. He is sick and finished. Everything going wrong. He goes into the car and tries to stay warm. He shuts his eyes for a while. He is listening to the storm roaring, the blast shaking the car.

Then after a while he is okay.

If the hitchhiker was here he would be outside, kneeling in the slush and the oil thanking God for all this, the storm and the fire, the wreckage, the impossibility and the winter night. Everything that is lost. Les thinks he should get down beside him. But Les needs to get himself and the car back to Edinburgh: He needs to raise money, get the car fixed. In a week he is going to go South to collect her, his skin and flesh and bones, his taste and touch and eyes are already alive just to see her again, to be driving towards her, to be with her, to be taking her home.

Not Drinking. Or Not

The first time Angela saw Eddie he was standing red-faced (from shyness and his holiday abroad) beside the public telephones and W.V.S. shop at the main entrance to the Royal Infirmary in Edinburgh where he had come to visit his mother. He was so good looking Angela forgot to buy the mints for Felicity, her friend, who was upstairs in ward 3C with a broken ankle, and went back up to the ward with nothing but joy and confusion followed by Eddie whose mother was in the next bed to Felicity.

So that's how Angela and Eddie first met. Nine years later she killed him with a hammer as he lay sleeping and drunk with the blood from her eyes and ears still on his knuckles.

It was because of this blood, and the state of the bones of her face and body, and her broken teeth, that she was two years in jail when she had thought it might be longer, even forever.

Their three children grew up. And although they understood why she, their mother, had killed their father, and although they themselves had been released from fear by her act, there was a tension, a formality, always to be between them, as if they could never deserve to relax or to be happy together. They were however, all four separately, capable of a shadowed kind of happiness with other people.

Angela dreamed of Eddie (at least she thought it might be Eddie). But it was never of the time of, nor of her involvement in, his death. Instead she dreamed of all the good times they had had the opportunity to have together and, it seemed to her, would have had, had those events and their possibility of joy and pleasure not always been surrounded by the fear that Eddie would drink too much and of what he would do then. She dreamed of those good opportunities and this way they became as they should have been. She and Eddie (if it was Eddie), would laugh and dance at the weddings and parties and when the occasion was over they would go home together in the night in happiness and exhaustion and any fear they felt was not of each other but instead of what might be waiting outside of them. And later, if in the darkness they awoke, they would whisper to each other and hold each other, shield and protect each other from whatever might surround them, that could close in on them sometime, any time of their lives.

Eventually she didn't dream anymore.

And mostly, but not always, nowadays, she believes that the person in the dreams was never Eddie at all.

Tonight Angela is in the far North at the wedding of her niece Catriona. It is July and the sun hardly going down between night and morning. The reception is in a marquee in the garden of Catriona's parents' house. Angela is standing near the bar trying not to look alone too long, trying to look as if she does not notice she is noticed by others who remind each other (outside of her hearing range) of what she did twenty years, nearly twenty years, not such a long time, ago.

Her younger sister Molly, Catriona's mother, (who at the age of sixteen had bitten off part of Eddie's ear as he tried to kick Angela on the ground), comes over with a man. He is wearing a dark grey suit, a white shirt and a tie coloured with bright creatures. His hair, which would have once been very dark, is mostly grey. He is smiling with what looks like his own (but wonderful) teeth.

"This is David, from my work," says Molly. "My sister, Angela. What will I get you both to drink?"

"A whisky. Any one at all. No water," says Angela.

"An orange juice or something like that please," he says.

Later Angela asks him, "Do you not drink?"

"No, not much, maybe something......, I mean, no. Actually nothing at all. I mean nothing anymore. Or not for a long time. I mean, I tried drinking when I was young. I felt I should. Should be able to. But it was no good. I always got really ill.

Really sick. Just nearly killed me with hardly any at all. So I could never drink. It never worked. Anything. So eventually I didn't bother any more. Or now and then I would because you feel different at that age not doing what everyone else does. What you want to do as well. To be like them. So you try again. Different drinks. Different advice. But it was always the same and I'd be sick for days even after just one or two sips and of course I'd be ashamed of myself as well. God. As if I was strange. Wrong in some way not being able to drink. I mean surely it is just as strange to be able to drink a lot with no ill effects because actually it's a poison, isn't it? And in the end, those that can drink a lot, they think they can drink anything they like because it doesn't show ill effects when they are young but it is actually doing them a lot of damage in the long run. So that's crazy. But it was me that felt like the strange one. That was the way it was then. Like you didn't belong or were soft in some way because you didn't. Or couldn't in my case. And sometimes I'd give it another try but as you get older, of course, even if you were alright with drink to begin with, as you get older the hangovers get worse. I think that's true. The effects. Your body is not so resilient so you cannot take so much and bounce back so easily and so if you start with no tolerance at all, as I did, obviously there is no point still trying ten or twenty years later, although sometimes I did. But it's still no good and it's not going to get any better. So I never try to drink at all nowadays. But of course it's much easier now. Not drinking. I mean you don't feel guilty or different anymore with the driving and the health and all that that people think about now. So it's more acceptable. I mean people accept it if you don't drink. They don't try to persuade you or go on at you like they once did. There are always so many folk now at anything not drinking so you don't feel as out of it or look as out of it as I once did. I mean it's not unusual and you don't feel odd. You can say no and no one bothers or even notices..... well, I know you did. But that's unusual. I mean, not unusual, but I mean sometimes, I mean, there is no harm, someone will ask, like you did. But not in the sense that they are pressurising you, not in the sense that they feel there is something wrong with you or that you are lacking something. It is just a question they might ask. But I suppose in a way it is funny that people still don't ask the reverse question: That's; why do you drink? Rather than why don't you? If things have changed I mean. But maybe because nowadays the person drinking is seen more as the person with a problem than the person who isn't so no one says anything. I mean, I don't mean, I mean, God, I'm sorry, I didn't mean, I mean, I wasn't trying to say, or even think, you've got a problem. Not at all. You obviously haven't. I mean, I can see, I'm sure, or that you were trying to say I've got one or anything like that, I mean, I know you were not trying to criticise me or anything. Good God no. Or put me down in any way or anything. And there is nothing wrong, I mean in itself, or in fact in drinking with drink anyway for most folk. Or anything anyway about drink. I mean, it doesn't matter. I mean, right now, or in fact anytime. I mean, not at all. Not a bit. Or you, well, especially, I mean, it's alright."

"Right." says Angela.

And the band is well warmed up now, the dancers stomping the wooden floor. She is looking at him. The warm night gathering around them. His blue eyes.

So Here Are Some Of The Things My Grandfather Left Me

When my grandfather retired he went home to live in a caravan on a farm in Lethen, Nairnshire, half a mile from where he had been born and where he had met and married my grandmother who was now dead.

My own father, who worked for the Social Work Department in Edinburgh, wanted my grandfather to come to Edinburgh, maybe to a sheltered house, but my grandfather, who had spent most of his working life as a mechanic moving from job to job and place to place, said he wanted to go home to Lethen and he already had the caravan so he did.

Although my grandfather had been a great mechanic, people said the very best, because of his restlessness he had never stayed in any job long enough to get on so he never had much money. But his son, my father, was different. He had not wanted to do the work his father did. He hated the cold, hard conditions, the physical struggle of his father's life so he had gone in a different direction. He had become a social worker. Indoors most of the time. Central heating. Clean clothes. Good pay. Settled, secure conditions.

My father had been very successful as a student. It was thought that he would rise fast but he developed a reputation, my mother said, for arrogance and tactlessness. Once, after he had been given some award and was being interviewed and congratulated by a local reporter, he had said that the standards and quality of work were so low amongst his colleagues that an award meant very little. It was easy, he said, to seem to do well when there was so little competition. My mother said my father had never really understood why this had annoyed so many people.

Although at one time I believed that my father and my grandfather did not get on, eventually I realised how much they really cared for each other: That my father admired my grandfather's skill with his hands and his impulsive life while my grandfather was proud of, delighted by, his son's extraordinary honesty and diplomatic innocence. Also any difficulties their differences might have caused had long ago been diffused by my mother who had, very early on, become the focus of their love for each other.

My mother was, is, an actress. She had her first roles as an adolescent in the sixties and, without ever having had ambition, vanity or even great acting ability, has continued to act in films or on television ever since. Not in the theatre. She is too lazy. Her real interest in life has never really been in acting at all but in people, company, friends, family. She and my father met at a party when they were very young and they have been together ever since. He is very quiet and serious and she is noisy and not at all. But they have stayed together and have seemed happy together. He intensely (and sometimes comically) following his conscience, she coasting along on her beauty, sociability and her enthusiasm for being alive. Her heavy smoking and carelessness about appearance, diet or exercise meant that these days she looks fairly rumpled but she is still beautiful in an ageing, hippyish way. And she is loved. Mostly. Completely uncompetitive she seems to make people feel relaxed and special. I had come home because she had been very ill. But she has survived and she says she will be ok. My father has stopped work to take care of her. She lost her hair, though she tells me it is growing back. She is wearing baseball caps all the time, even with evening dress, never allowing the illness to let her miss a night out.

I hadn't worked out who I was. (I certainly never seemed to make people feel relaxed). Perhaps like my grandfather without the skill, like my father without the responsibility, like my mother but without the beauty. I was always restless and not happy. I'd spent the last ten years since I left school working my way across some of the world: Europe, America, Australia and eventually Hong Kong, where I'd stayed longest. The best parts of my life so far had been when I was leaving somewhere or someone. I'd had few relationships and none for more than a few weeks and none that I regretted being over.

Now I was back in Edinburgh for a while. I was not staying with my mother and father which was always difficult for us all, but in a shared flat at the top of Leith Walk and working in a bar most nights. I was thinking of applying to train as a nurse or something. But none of my ambitions so far had ever lasted long enough for me to fill in the application forms.

My grandfather phoned me from the farm.

He said, "Jessie. Are you coming up here for your birthday? When will you get here? How is your mother doing? Is she making a go of it do you think? Tell them I'm doing well up here. Did you know I've got a dog? You'll see her when you get here. When's your birthday exactly? Wednesday is it? Get here as early as you can on Tuesday."

"I'll be there", I said. "Definitely Tuesday. Ready for Wednesday. I'm looking forward to it. I've not been with you for my birthday for years."

"Great," he said, "Great, great. And I've got a surprise for you, Jessie. Just wait and see."

"Oh Good. I wish it was Tuesday already."

Ever since I was a little girl my grandfather had made surprises for me for my birthday. Because I was an only child he put a lot of work and time into them. Sometimes months. Once I heard a friend of my parents saying that these surprises would have suited a boy much better than me. But my grandfather and I, and my parents, knew she was wrong. That these things he had made for me had been perfect. At least until I was thirteen. I think then he had realised (or had been helped to realise by my mother) that these surprises might not suit a teenager tortured by all the usual, and some extra, teenage things. The last surprise, when I was thirteen, had been a three feet high, remote controlled robot. This robot, called Robert, was powered by a diesel engine. He walked about, burping and smoking, on two short legs. His body was a huge inverted aluminium pot. He had flashing car indicator eyes and jointed moving arms with small shovels on the ends like scaled down JCB's. Unfortunately he was extremely powerful and hard to control. Unpredictable. In his short life he demolished a greenhouse, a neighbour's decorative wall, lots of plants, flowers, garden gnomes, statuary and a passing motor bike. Robert's end came when my grandfather was renting a place in Newport. (Robert had been banned from our house by then). Something to do with the stopping mechanism jammed and Robert walked straight down to the bottom of the garden and through the heavy safety fence. He fell sixteen feet into the Firth of Tay. For years I liked to imagine that he kept walking east, out underneath the sea, to emerge, trailing seaweed, onto a beach in Norway, although I also knew that, even if his engine could have kept going underwater, he would have run out of diesel after about thirty miles.

Another time, it was my twelfth birthday, my grandfather constructed a series of events in a yard he had in Lanark. To start this series I had to pull a red ribbon. A wheel turned, weights fell, water poured, jetted, flowed, dynamos sparked, fuse wires were lit and burned, rockets went off and clouds of coloured smoke mushroomed yellow, blue, green and red. There were drums, clatters, bells and, after all this had gone on for twenty minutes, the finale: A huge four foot high catherine wheel, flaming and spinning while a recording of happy birthday, or most of it, was played through a six foot high loudspeaker at exactly the same time as the police arrived. Even my grandfather was surprised at the spectacularity of his creation which had been seen, we were told, five miles away.

But this coming birthday I was going to be twenty eight years old. I was ready again for my grandfather's surprises. I drove North up the A9 to Carrbridge then across the Dava Moor to Lethen.

The farm where my grandfather lived was well off the road. I had taken my mother's car so I could do shopping for him. And get away fast myself. The caravan was at the back of the farm through a lot of mud and several cars that people had brought to him for a second or final opinion. He loved old cars. When he was brought one he would lay his hands on the bonnet (if it had one) and go somehow dreamy. He would gaze at rusty dying wrecks like children look at Christmas parcels. My mother called him the car whisperer.

When I pulled up at the caravan the first thing I saw was the dog. I should have known. A black and white collie with only one front leg, the left one. Also only one ear and maybe only one eye, again on the left. (The right eye was closed so I could not tell if there was an eye in there or not.) But it was as menacing as any farm collie I'd ever been threatened by. And energetic. It had a very stumpy tail for a collie which it was wagging along with the growling.

My grandfather came out of the caravan in a cloud of smoke. There would be some pals in there.

"Jessie. Good to see you. You've met Mor then I hear," he shouted above the dog. "What's left of her anyway."

He said this with great pride. Mor as a younger dog, he told me, was a working collie who, when she wasn't out on the hills, used to chase any car, lorry, bike or bus that passed the end of her farm road. (This was another farm over towards Forres.) Then one day Mor caught up with the school bus and was dragged and trapped up underneath the wheel arch. No one heard anything because of the usual din the children were making inside. It was not until the bus went back to the garage that the driver found the dog because of the blood dripping down the wheel when the bus stopped. My grandfather was there, fixing another vehicle. He took the unconscious and dying dog to the vet. As well as what was missing, or left behind on the roads, there were big gashes in her chest and broken ribs and bones. The vet was going to inject her. Kill her. But the dog woke up. She looked at my grandfather through the blood covering the eye she had left and my grandfather asked the vet to try to give her a chance. Which the vet did. And although Mor was only four years old when the accident happened she went on to be one of the oldest known collies in Nairnshire. She lived till she was twenty three, outliving my grandfather by many years. Mor, to the end of her life, seemed totally unaware of her injuries and could never understand why the sheep could now run so much faster than she could.

My grandfather held open the door of the caravan. Inside, through the fug, were all the pals, eating pies, drinking tea and smoking: Jeems, Maggie Allan, Walter Seaton, John Dow the farmer, The Other John, Old Peter and the Captain.

My grandfather said, "We'll need to wait till dark. But have a pie and a cup of tea then I'll show you our latest contraption."

"I'll just have the tea, not the pie. I'm a vegetarian, Granpa," I said.

"So was the poor creature in that pie," said Walter Seaton.

"Now don't be teasing her after she's come all this way to see me, Walter," said my grandfather. "And it is so nearly her birthday."

After the tea we went out to one of the barns. Up the stair in the loft my grandfather showed me this huge telescope he had fixed jutting out through the roof. He must have used every penny he had, plus a lot of favours, to get this. Round all the walls were books on astronomy and charts of the skies and stars.

"The hole was already in the roof," said my grandfather. "I was up here going to fix it for John Dow. Then I saw the stars through the gap and I got the idea for the telescope. I wish I'd started sooner in life but never mind. Wait till dark. Midnight.

Your birthday. You'll see."

We went back to the caravan. He showed me my bunk. He had made it up with fresh sheets and pillows because usually Mor the dog slept there when there were no guests. Actually I discovered in the middle of the night that Mor slept there even when there was a guest.

That night is really dark. Outside it is country silent which is just as noisy as the city only more spaced out, articulate and disturbing: Things killing and being killed out there.

In the loft my grandfather has cranked the telescope out into the darkness. The Captain is attaching a metal box and headphones to the body of the apparatus. Mor is attacking and chewing the hem of his trousers. My grandfather and the pals are talking, laughing, drinking and studying the sky through the telescope, turn about. Waiting for midnight.

Just before the time comes my grandfather takes a look through the telescope. Everyone goes quiet.

He whispers, "There it is."

He stands back and I look through the eye pieces. I can see nothing focused at first. Only soft colours, whites, pale greens, yellows, blues. They are moving slowly. Not away or across but like some living thing breathing. My grandfather gives me the headphones he has plugged into the metal box at the side of the telescope.

"Can you see anything, Jessie? Hear anything?" he says.

He is trying to stay calm, but his suppressed excitement is affecting Mor who is running round and round the barn barking and raising clouds of dust. And now the pals are all on their feet, Jeems filling their glasses ready for a toast. But I can hear nothing and recognise nothing in the pulsating colours. Instead I feel my unhappiness, my failure, (though not for this), rising from my stomach, into my chest, swelling in my throat. What if I were to fall apart? My grandfather and the pals and Mor are now making a great din, jumping and dancing about. I can hear them but muffled by the headphones. I want to be happier for their sake. I don't want to let them down.

"Can you hear it, Jessie? Can you see it? Can you, Jessie? Can you see it?" they are shouting, the dog barking.

But I can't.

I can't.

And then I can. Very distant at first. Then louder. Then louder and louder.

Caaa-ushshshshsh shshshshshsss. Caa-ushshshshsh shshshshshssss. Ca-ushshshshsh shshshshshssssss.

"It's a sea, Jessie. It's a sea," my grandfather is shouting. "It's a beach."

And it is. Millions and millions and millions of years out there in space is a sea, a tide, the waves running on that beach, Caa-ushshshsh--shshshshsh, Ca-ushshshshsh--shshshshsh, Caaa-ushshshshsh-----shshshshsh, over and over, louder, louder, louder.

"I can hear it, Granpa," I shout to him, but I cannot hear my words in the crashing of the waves over me, my face and neck are wet with the spray, the salt taste in my mouth, blinding my eyes. I shout to my grandfather again, but they are all singing now and I know no one will hear me anymore when I cannot even hear myself.

Later that night Mor wakes me when she climbs in the bunk. She has a strong dungy smell from the byres where she has been chasing rats. I can hear my grandfather and Maggie Allan snoring at the far end of the caravan. When we came down from the loft he stumbled on the stairs.

"Too much happiness for an old man," he said.

"Too much whisky for an old man," I said.

"Ah," he said. "Well."

So here are some of the things my grandfather left me. A caravan. A dog. Some books on Astronomy. A telescope and a 200,000 mile, twenty year old, red and rust Ford Escort. The caravan is my home for now (and also a drinking and smoking den for every old scoundrel in the district of Lethen who is thrown out by his or her relatives each day). The dog looks like only half a dog, but you could also say that Mor is nearer to two dogs because of an excess of personality. I have started reading the books. But only just. I haven't looked through the telescope again since my grandfather died. I'm still not sure how scientific an instrument it is.

And the Ford Escort: I am surprised how much I know about cars. I can fix them. It's like I have some of my grandfather's magic in me after all. The skill. I like this old car even when it breaks down because I know I can get it going again. All those hours I spent when I was a child chatting to my grandfather's boots, which was all I could see when he was underneath some machine, I must have been learning things without noticing. And John Dow has an old Land Rover lying in the field here which he says I can have a go at as well if I want.

What my grandfather also left me, though no one has exactly said so, is seven decrepit and delinquent old pals, including Maggie Allan who I see every day. When she was here last night she was weeping again for my grandfather.

"I should have married him when he asked me," she sobbed.

"Well," I said, not so sure it was marriage he was actually after. I seem to have learnt a lot more about men in little more than a third of Maggie's time. Still. Sometimes when people die some of the things they leave you are very hard to define.

Today I phoned my mother.

"How is the hair coming on?" I ask her.

"Kind of fluffy," she says. "Like a baby. And how are you doing up there with all the old codgers? Have you met any younger folk? When are you coming back to Edinburgh?"

"Well," I say. "I think I'll be here for a while yet. I've got this dog now to take care of. I can't really see Mor in a top flat in Leith when the whole of Lethen is hardly big enough for her. And I'm starting a job in a bar on Monday. Also Walter Seaton has asked me to marry him. I'm thinking of saying yes."

"God," says my mother. "That drunken old rascal. I know

you're not serious. If you'd said Jeems I might have half believed you. At least Jeems doesn't take his teeth out every time he wants to dance like Walter Seaton did at your grandfather's funeral."

"Oh that's not fair on Walter," I tell her. "It was only for the fast dances. He kept them in the rest of the time. But I'll tell you though who I've seen a lot of is your cousin Lorraine's niece, Polly Johnston. Remember she came with Lorraine to Grandpa's funeral. Polly says that Grandpa and her grandmother were kind of third cousins. So we're all related. Us and her and Lorraine. And she's great company, Polly. She makes me laugh. She got me the job in the hotel."

After our phone call I go outside and sit on the plastic crate and watch Mor watching something I can't see underneath the caravan. Waiting for whatever it is to run out. It'll be safe enough either way. Mor never manages to catch anything anymore.

My mother says that when someone dies, usually everything they leave, chairs, houses, cars, friends, countries, ideas, everything, seems to shrink. Some things for a while and some forever. But in my grandfather's case this has not been true. Everything he had looks to me like it's still the same as it was before. Or even more so. Maybe it is just that the kind of things he had are not so easily shrunk.

And talking of more, I'm supposed to be meeting Polly tonight and it's been at least a few days since I had a bath. I should go up to the farm house and see if John Dow will let me use his. I'll take Mor with me to guard the bathroom door. There's no lock and the last time I had a bath there John Dow kept bursting in with fresh towels.

That night that I saw the beach through the telescope Maggie and I had to help my grandfather into his bunk. We put the blankets over him and I kissed him goodnight.

"It's great to be here, Granpa," I told him. "Thank you for my birthday surprise."

"You know it isn't a real beach, don't you Jessie?" he said.

I said, "I know, Granpa. I know."

But later when I was lying in the darkness in my own bunk, still not sleeping, what I knew for the very first time was that my Granpa was dying. And that maybe my mother wasn't getting any better either. Maybe she would die too.

Not very long ago all I wanted to do was go on long journeys with no one to meet me at the other end. To be where no one knew me. But now things are different. I don't want those kind of journeys any more. I want to be here for a while, feeding my dog, phoning my mother. Getting drunk now and then with Polly. Whatever happens next.

Different Lives. Christine Johnstone And Rosie Stuart

Mary Stuart killed her three children and then killed herself. This was a long time ago when I was a child so I can hardly remember. Only that the world became a different place as if a dark haar came down and my own mother (who might herself have been a ghost out there far into that mist, that distance, so dim my remembrance of her that day and only her touch, dry and warm, still alive with me) held my hand very tightly till the bones were crushed together in comfort as we walked down the long track towards some gathering that was itself a consequence of what Mary Stuart had done where the adults talked in voices that were thickened and lost and would cease altogether when they remembered that we, the still living children, were there. But that silence still seems to me worse than anything we could have heard.

And then, years later, when I was still at home but almost leaving, I heard my mother say that Mary Stuart came from an unlucky family. Later again my sister, studying psychology at the University in Aberdeen, told me from what she had learned might have happened to make Mary Stuart do what she did. Then, five years after this, when she, my beautiful, until then always happy, generous sister, had her first child, we sat together for days in her dark rooms, the curtains drawn shut against the light (as if in the time of a death), and matched and compared the awfulness and fear of her own depression to whatever it might have been that Mary Stuart had felt.

And it seemed as if every new thing that I learned, and every new way the world could be seen, could only be tested, could only be made valid, by it seeming to bring me closer to something about those four deaths and I, hundreds of miles, and twenty, forty, fifty years from that event, would find myself in cities and trains or rooms that were temporary and unfamiliar staring back into the darkness of what Mary Stuart had done and remembering what my mother had said: Did my mother believe that bad luck travels down through blood and flesh and bone? And is that, which we had learned to call superstition in my mother, what we begin to believe in again although we call them curses no more but genes that travel down from our ancestors to us and our children and guide us to similar fates instead of those we might have hoped for?

But I have never had children. By the time I grew up being alone was just something I was good at like other people are good at swimming. Or singing. I was anyway never someone that the boys watched or the girls phoned in the evenings or gathered around in the schooldays. It was not that I was rejected or hurt or bullied, it was just that I spent most of my spare time, if I spent it with anyone at all, with my sister or my parents or my dog Jim. Especially with Jim (whose company I probably preferred to any other). When the people I was in school with started going to parties and being out together I was already somehow missed out, although I did not notice myself missing at the time (and even if I had I think I would have chosen to stay missing). It was not until much later that I felt any absence, any loneliness. Maybe after my sister married, but not exactly then either. No. If I have ever missed anyone at all as time has gone by, I suppose it has been Rosie.

Rosie was the oldest of Mary Stuart's three children. We were the same age and she was six when she died, but those memories I have of her are clear and sharp. The last of these (although this might not have been the last time I saw her) is of a dark day, very dark, wet and muddy. Maybe it is winter, late afternoon, that's how it feels. Rosie is wearing a coat, but open, over a dress printed with flowers. Her face is mottled white and blood red in the cold. We are together at the top of the farm track (where later I am to walk down with my mother). We face each other, the whiteness of her teeth chattering with mine in the wind and her lips swollen dark and blue.

"It's awful cold the day, Christine," she says. "Do you feel it too?"

Now, sixty years later, I am sitting on the bench at the bend of the river at the deep Whinnieknowe pool where children and dogs swim in the summer. And because I have been away from this town for so long and have hardly ever been back till I could come back here to stay, when I meet people of my own age, out walking dogs, or when I am at a house, or at some event, it can be a long time before we realise that we were children together, at school together, in the same class, and it is even then (even after we have identified each other by place and name) a long time, if ever, before I see in this old person before me the child I knew when I myself was a child.

But I would recognise Rosie.

This is how I expect we will meet again.

I will look up from the bench where I have been watching the river and she will be coming down the path between the trees. A fat labrador walks before her. She has grown old like me, her body solid like mine, but I will know it is Rosie. Now she sees me. She is coming towards me. She recognises me. She is hurrying now, Rosie my friend, having lived her whole life and all the things that we do, the summers and the winters, the whole world turning; having lived our whole lives, different lives, in the sounds of the night and the light coming in in the mornings; having lived our whole lives, different lives, having never died, having never been killed by her mother.

Lethen

My mother and father first met in 1940. My father was working in Lethen for a farmer called William Forbes when the new district nurse drove up in her Morris.

The war was on. My father was not away fighting because he was in a reserved occupation. (He told me it was because he was too small. But nothing my father told me turned out to be true.)

So my mother, eventually, married my father and came to live on the farm. But she would always be a nurse. In the evenings after tea, if we had been good, my sisters and I would get to watch my mother lance the boils on the arms and necks of my father and the other farm workers.

In the kitchen the man would lay his arm, if that was where the boil was, on the table, and my mother would lay her kit handy alongside; cotton wool, disinfectant, a bowl of boiling water and a razor. The children would gather round and push to get a good view. The best position was standing on a chair on the opposite side of the table from the boil. My father would bring over the Tilley lamp and pump it up. The man would turn away from my mother and talk to my father. (When it was my father himself who had the boil he would sweat and shout, "Good God, Annie, you're killing me!" But of course then there were no other men around).

While my mother was working on the boil the man and my father would be talking about William Forbes and how mean he was. My father brought us up to see William Forbes as the enemy. He told us to stand our ground if we saw William Forbes coming so that he would have to walk round us. This was not dangerous because William Forbes was small and thin. My father told me that William Forbes had once been a very tall man but that he had shrunk himself to save money on clothes and food.

In fact my father was smaller than William Forbes but my father was very fat with a red face. And he was small for a different reason. When he was a child he had had three brothers who were all older than him so he was given their old clothes to wear when they outgrew them. My father never had anything new. Then, when he was nine, his auntie Jean bought him a suit. He really loved that suit, his own, the newness, first hand, so he stopped growing so that the suit would always fit. He said that he had married my mother in that suit. He said that if he had not stopped himself growing to fit that suit he would have been eight feet tall.

Once the boil was open my mother would clean out the poison and swab out the gap with disinfectant. At the very moment the disinfectant went in we would switch our eyes from the boil to the man's face when the man might hesitate in mid sentence. But my father would leap in with a remark and the man would listen intently. I noticed this solidarity of males very early on and I looked forward to the day when I would have boils. I was still then on ringworm and hen fleas.

My mother loved being a nurse and after my father died she became a nurse again. This time she delivered babies to women she had delivered as babies. The first time it had been by lamplight in cottages and farms up the country. The second time the light was electric light in Nairn hospital where you went to either die or to be born; anything more serious and you were sent to Inverness fifteen miles away. My mother delivered over two hundred babies the first time she was district nurse and they all lived. She would point out grim determined wild grown men on Nairn High Street and say, "That's one of my babies."

My mother had been trained as a nurse at the Royal Infirmary in Edinburgh. She had gone there from the Isle of Skye when she was seventeen. When we were children she talked often of Edinburgh and our favourite bedtime stories were of brain operations, amputations, suicides and her first district as a midwife in the Grassmarket and Cowgate. She had come North to Lethen because she wanted more independence, her own district. When she saw Lethen she loved it. My father said God made Lethen so that people could have an idea of what heaven would be like. I asked my father why there were so many wicked people like William Forbes in Lethen if it was so close to Heaven. My father said that William Forbes was getting his last chance.

Fourteen years ago, when my mother was about seventy, I phoned her up one night.

I said, "I'm thinking of coming up to see you this weekend."

She said, "You can't come up. I'm shutting the house for a few weeks."

I said, "Why? Where are you going?"

She said, "Well. I'm going into hospital tomorrow."

"Hospital?" I said. "What for?"

"Well," she said, "I've got a wee lump."

"A WEE LUMP! GOD! IT'S CANCER! A WEE LUMP! WHY DIDN'T YOU TELL ME! GOD! YOU COULD DIE! IT'S CANCER. I'M COMING UP. THIS IS AWFUL! HOW COULD YOU NOT TELL ME SOONER!"

"What a state to get into," she said. "It's just a wee operation. No wonder I didn't tell you. I don't want you coming up here, carrying on. It's hardly anything. A wee lump, two minutes it'll take. And anyway," she said, "why would you come up? They'll not let you watch."

So it was cancer and very bad so she had the operations and lost a considerable percentage of herself.

"Which I never miss," she says, and anytime I phone her she is not in. There is a gang of them up there drinking tea and whisky and playing cards. All single women. The men are all dead. Even when I go up she is out every night. Her babies' babies are having babies.

Donald Ker was born on the Arr Farm, Lethen, Nairnshire at 4.30am on 24th May, 1944, in the upstairs bedroom from where you can see one hundred miles into the North. His mother was a midwife from the Island of Lewis. His father, a tenant farmer, was downstairs in the kitchen with his pals. Donald Ker was brought up by three German prisoners of war, two sisters and a collie dog called Lucky in the last days of Clydesdale horses and no electricity. In 1952 his father bought a Ferguson tractor, but then drowned in 1957 so Donald Ker joined the Royal Navy where he was introduced to art, especially Gauguin. The Navy encouraged this interest and sent him, under guard, from HMS Condor in Arbroath to Duncan of Jordonston School of Art in Dundee every Thursday night and, when his drawing improved, discharged him, amicably and not totally dis-honourably, in 1963. He then dug holes for the Hydro Board, from Skye to Turriff, till 1965 when he went to the Art School in Aberdeen where he fell in love (unrequited) with ceramics.

In 1971, in Edinburgh, by accident, he started work as a baker, then potter, at Garvald Centre where he has been ever since, mainly due to happiness.

Donald Ker has three Children, Esther, Daniel and Luke (but no dog). He was very lucky, in 1971, to meet his wonderful, beautiful, ex-wife Ruth, and lucky that a woman as smashing as herself managed to live with him until 1986 when she divorced him.